D1240697

# FREDERICK MOODY

## AND THE
## SECRETS OF SIX SUMMIT LAKE

## JEANNIE RIVERA

GRIFFIN
CHILDREN'S BOOKS
AN IMPRINT OF SILHASTAL PUBLICATIONS

GRIFFIN CHILDREN'S BOOKS

**Published by:**

Griffin Children's Books (An Imprint of Bicoastal Publications

**www.bicoastalpublications.com**

9924 Universal Blvd, Ste. 224
Orlando, Florida 32819

Edited and formatted by: J.C. Mastro
Cover art and design by: J.C. Mastro

**www.jcmastroauthor.com**

# PRAISE FOR FREDERICK MOODY

"A winning set up—fun, smoothly paced, and engaging with a vivid mountain town setting that allows the novel to quietly shine."

- *TheBookLifePrize*

"As an author and children's fiction fan, Frederick Moody brings back memories of reading adventure mysteries up in a backyard tree, being a junior detective, and chasing imaginary monsters through the woods. As a dad, I love how Fred captures the imagination and exemplifies friendship and acceptance."

*– J.C. Mastro, Author of Academy Bound*

*For my four sons:*

*Adam, Matthew, Thomas, and Jason*

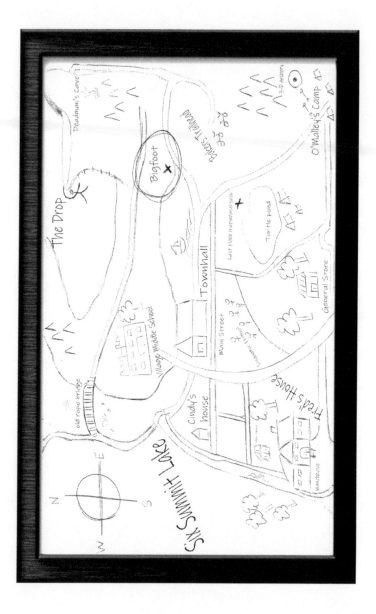

Bigfoot stomped through the woods outside the village of Six Summit Lake on Wednesday, the 24th of September, uprooting foliage and crushing campsites. And by Friday, that crapweasal Luke was missing... Which may or may not have been Frederick Moody's fault.

# ONE

F REDERICK MOODY SAT AT the dining room table, picking at his dinner. His best friend, Cindy, hadn't spoken to him in months. But proving Bigfoot was real would fix everything. Only—his presentation was the next day, and he didn't have the evidence he needed.

Static blared through Granddad's radio, which sat on the credenza across the room. "Sheriff, You there?"

Granddad set the dinner fork next to his plate, eying the steaming pot roast, and sighed. His dark blue uniform still looked as freshly pressed as it had early that morning. He pushed away from the table, the chair's legs scraping across the polished dining room floor.

"Sheriff?"

More static.

"We got a situation..."

He crossed the room and snatched the walkie-talkie from its cradle off the credenza. "Moody, here," Granddad said. He sounded as annoyed as he looked. "What is it, Joe? Just sat down to supper."

"Sorry, sir," Joe's voice echoed through the speaker. "We got a hiker not checked in. Set camp 'round Baker's Ridge."

"10-4." Granddad grabbed his sheriff's hat from the side table. "Go up there, Joe, and see what's what."

"Kids said they saw something...big and fur-covered—"

That got Fred's attention.

Granddad smashed the side button on the radio. "Report to my office when you're through."

"Yes, sir."

Fred's heart sped up. Being the sheriff's grandson had its advantages, like learning about the missing hiker before any other sixth grader in town.

Granddad snapped the radio into the pouch on his duty belt, snatched his plate from the table, and pushed through the door to the kitchen, "Be back in a few hours."

Fred shoved the last of his meat and potatoes into his mouth, listening to Granddad bang around in the refrigerator. He had to hurry. He'd take the back way to avoid the deputies.

As soon as he heard Granddad's boots creak up the stairs, Fred bolted through the foyer, grabbed his coat, and slipped out the garage door. He hurried past the orange Bigfoot Crossing sign outside Sasquatch Summit General Store, heading toward the trailhead.

Six Summit Lake was famous for its Bigfoot sightings and twice-a-year Sasquatch Festivals. Anyone who grew up there knew the basics. Between school plays, gift shops, and all the peepers (visitors come to town to peep at the leaves, the mountain people, and, of course, the Bigfoot), it was impossible to avoid Bigfoot legends there.

Still, most people didn't believe the stories were true. But Fred did. And not just because his granddad and granduncle were part of "The Bigfoot Sighting of '72." He felt it in his bones even if Granddad insisted "he ain't seen nothing out in them woods."

Didn't matter. Fred would prove the creature was real.

A police cruiser sped by with its lights on.

"Crapsticks," Fred swore.

As he moved across the general store's parking lot, a couple pushed through the door. The woman wore a big goofy grin. She shook a glass globe with Bigfoot standing in the center, snow floating around him. She tucked a red-brown, scraggly-haired stuffy beneath her arm.

The man carried an *Adirondack Journal* newspaper he must've purchased inside with the headline Fred had read earlier. "Festival Extended to Three Days. Revenue Expected to Skyrocket."

"Says here," the man tapped the lower right corner of the front page, "record lows expected this weekend. Maybe we need extra blankets, or—"

"We'll be fine. My weather app didn't say it would be that cold. Quit worrying."

"Amateurs," Fred muttered under his breath. It was a mistake many out-of-towners made. Those apps never showed actual temperatures at the summits.

The woman gave the snow globe another good shake and hopped in the passenger side of an old blue Honda Civic. The back window had decals of Bigfoot chasing a family with a chunky kid falling behind that said, "Be Nice to Fat People, They May Save Your Life," which was completely obnoxious. Fred couldn't understand why people were so mean. He examined the rest of the stickers covering the bumper. "Bigfoot Hunters," "Sasquatch Sighters," "Yeti Yellers," and Fred's favorite, "Bigfoot doesn't believe in you either." Great. Fred scoffed. Annoying *peepers*. "Good luck," he mumbled sarcastically before turning to head for the trail.

Fred settled into a dense thicket where the foliage was high and perfect. He could stay for hours, and no one would find him unless they climbed into the bushes. It was an ideal spot to spy on the crime scene. He scanned the undergrowth where he hid. Animal tracks cut the ground up. Small paw prints he couldn't identify, and hoof marks from a deer. Regular stuff one would expect to find in the forest—along with a smashed soda can and a few discarded cigar butts.

He was already in place and within earshot when his granddad's deputies arrived. They picked their way through the slapped-together camp. Near the makeshift fire pit, more empty cans and chip bags littered the ground. A cooler was tossed over. A camp chair lay on its side, mangled. Shopping bags were torn open, remnants of chicken bones spilling out. As Fred shifted to get a better look, a dry branch crunched beneath his feet. He froze, hoping they hadn't heard him.

Officer Joe snapped a picture. "What do you think, Dad?"

"Call me *Sergeant Finney*, when we're working, Joe." The Senior Sergeant Roy Finney removed his hat and ran a hand through his thinning hair. "Don't know what to think, but it's not—"

"Bigfoot." The corner of Officer Joe's mouth twitched, revealing a dimple on his cheek. Then he pressed his lips together as if trying not to smile.

Finney Senior shot him a harrowed look. "No such thing as Bigfoot. You know better than that. Probably a bear or something." He crouched in front of the shredded tent and motioned with his hand, swiping sideways. "These look like claw marks. And look at all the food stuff. Careless."

Officer Joe squatted next to Finney Senior. "A bear?"

"I spotted paw prints back a little way."

Joe shook his head. "This got Bigfoot written all over it. Those kids said the creature tossed a guy over its shoulders and ran off into the woods."

"There are no Bigfeet."

"Bigfoots, Dad."

Fred laughed. He couldn't help it.

"What was that?" Joe shone his light toward the bushes.

Fred held his breath, but Joe didn't seem to notice him.

Finney Senior growled. "Nothing's out here. And you need to stop making crazy suggestions like that, you hear? We got a missing hiker. He's in them woods somewhere, and we'll find him."

"But the kids—"

"Them boys don't know what they seen. And the last thing we need is more Bigfeet hysteria in Six Summit Lake."

"Would bring in more peepers."

"Peepers! Every nut, psycho, hunter, and TV crew would turn up trying to catch a sight, and they'd all be in the way. That's how folks get hurt. We need to keep those crazies out of these mountains until we find the hiker, understand?"

Joe shrugged. "Looks like Bigfoot to me."

He snapped one last picture and followed Finney Senior down the path.

Fred liked Officer Joe. He was the only person in town who didn't think his research was stupid. And Mayor Baxter's crazy old brother Bill, but his support did nothing to boost Fred's credibility.

When the officers disappeared, Fred emerged from the bushes. He circled the fire pit, snapped pictures of his own, and crawled into the leaning tent. A crumpled sleeping bag and battery-operated camping lantern sat beside a blow-up pillow. He peered out, made sure Officer Joe and his dad were long gone, and then flipped the switch on the lantern.

He'd spied on dozens of investigations and searches without being caught. Fred shined the light around the camp and took out his Go-Pro to film the scene for his YouTube channel. As he stepped into the tree line, he caught a whiff of an obnoxious odor—a cross between sweat, smoke, and dead things.

He followed the smell and the torn-up dirt and debris going in the opposite direction, expecting the odor to get worse. It didn't. He rounded a tall birch tree. In the dirt, clear as a freezing winter's morning, was a huge indentation.

Fred dropped to his knees, the light flickering in his shaking hands.

A footprint.

Counting the six toe marks, he ran his fingers across the ridges in the dirt. The imprint was as deep as the length of a hand, and the tore-up ground where the pad of the foot landed was deeper than the rest. Bigfoot had walked right through those trees. And Fred had finally found the proof he needed.

# TWO

F RED WAS STILL AWAKE Thursday morning when the alarm to get up for school went off. He'd worked all night in the Watchcave, putting together his presentation. The Watchcave was where he monitored sightings, maintained his YouTube channel, and constructed his inventions. It was his own secret lab, his Fortress of Solitude, his Batcave.

Okay, Aunt Faye let him convert the two-car garage to a workspace so he'd stop bringing all his junk in the house. But it was his.

He'd fixed the space nicely, even if it looked like a cross between a police investigation room and a computer graveyard. A world map studded with pushpins covered one entire wall. He used different colored strings: red, blue, green, and yellow to signify the type of evidence reported. Eyewitnesses, footprints, photographs, and bones. Layers of photos and newspaper clippings buried the details of the countries on the map.

Blackboard paint coated the opposite wall with scrawled chalk notes. An oval boardroom table cluttered the center of the room with half-dissected computers piled on top, and a mess of Amazon boxes shoved beneath. On the back wall above his black executive desk, a terrain map of the summits hung beside a cork board plastered with green hazy pictures Fred took with his homemade infrared camera. And he'd repurposed the old coat hooks and boot racks next to the side door for his archery equipment.

Fred's knee bounced as he tapped the keyboard, squinting through his glasses at the dual computer monitors. His eyes were tired, but nervous energy strummed through his body. He wouldn't have been able to sleep even if he tried. Sightings were happening again.

He glanced at the old newspaper clipping on the desk of his grand-uncle and Mayor Baxter wearing ridiculous bell-bottom pants and tight, button-down paisley shirts. Headline: "Six Summit Lake High School Students Spot Bigfoot."

Granddad's cigar smoke wafted through the open window. Fred held his breath. He didn't have a bedtime or anything. When his parents were away on a dig, which was always, he lived on his own, mostly. Granddad spent every waking moment in his office. And Aunt Faye paid him no mind if he passed his classes and stayed out of trouble. That was assuming he hadn't blown up the garage with one of his inventions. It only happened once, and it was a minor explosion.

"Frederick?" Granddad called from outside.

Fred didn't want his granddad to know about his spying on the campsite. Not yet.

He shoved the article beneath his keyboard, scattering the collection of postcards from his parents he kept there. Two slipped off the back of the desk and fluttered to the floor. "Um, yeah?"

"Shut the infonet down and dress for school."

Fred crawled beneath the desk, navigating the tangled mess of wires to retrieve the postcards. "10-4."

Granddad's heavy boots crunched on the gravel driveway. The cruiser's door slammed shut, and the engine roared.

Fred scanned the room for his favorite Fortnite tee. It lay on the floor in the corner. It passed the sniff test. He tugged the crumpled shirt over his head, knocking random twigs from the night before out of his hair. Dark curls stuck up from his head like springs in every direction. Black-rimmed glasses slipped from the bridge of his nose. Jeans still looked good. The circles under his eyes did not. But he'd catch up on sleep later. The day was too important—and he was already running late.

Fred swung an overstuffed book bag over his right shoulder and hopped on his skateboard. But when he rolled by the vacant house next door, his stomach felt empty. He was never late when Cindy lived there. He missed her banging on his door in the mornings, walking to school together, and sharing gooey chocolate cookies from Bigfoot Beans coffee shop. He still remembered the first day she'd moved in during the summer before kindergarten. He had been sitting in his room watching the men carry furniture inside when she looked at him and waved. That night she shined flashlight beams at his window. It was their own Batsignal. They spent the summer tinkering with inventions, playing in the woods, and splashing around in the lake. And had been best friends ever since.

But then she and her mom moved away across town last year. And almost at the same time, she stopped speaking to him because his research was stupid. But that would change, and he'd win his best friend back. He wouldn't even be upset if she still called his Watchcave "the Fortress of Geekiness." Actually, he kind of liked it.

The town buzzed with people, and the festival didn't even start until the following night. Fred rolled on his skateboard past the boat launch and marina, squinting into the sun beaming off the sparkling water. Speeders and pontoons swayed in the slips waiting for one last voyage before the freeze set in. It wouldn't be long. Burning wood chips and the smell of approaching snow already filled the air.

He turned on Main Street, intending to pick up speed to make the hill to Six Summit Lake Village Middle School, but a crowd had gathered in front of town hall. He zigzagged, whizzing in and out of the cluster of people, and stopped when his granddad and Mayor Baxter stepped out of the building.

Granddad stood a head taller than the mayor, wearing his clean-shaven serious face. His uniform was perfectly pressed with creases running down the pant legs. Fred eyed his own wrinkled shirt and winced. For an old guy, his granddad had a good head of hair, brown with silver running through the sides. Fred had his eyes. Serious, with irises so dark it was hard to make out the pupils, which was unnerving. He could never tell when Granddad was watching him.

When the mayor stepped to a portable lectern, Granddad crossed his arms over his chest like one of those bouncers on television, daring anyone to pass him.

The local news crew shoved a microphone beneath the mayor's bushy mustache. He looked his usual self, with yesterday's whiskers, blue jeans, pale brown T-shirt, and muddy sneakers as if he'd been working on his farm. Even for a press conference, the guy didn't dress up.

Mayor Baxter adjusted his ball cap, pushing a few strands of silvery blond hair back beneath its mesh, and grinned. "The Six Summit Lake Police Department and New York State Police will locate the campers. We have the finest team of law enforcement officers and rescue crews in the Adirondacks."

"Think it was Bigfoot?" a reporter asked, his lips drawing up at the corners.

The guy wore a black leather jacket over slacks, and must have been from out of town. Fred didn't recognize him.

"Campers get lost in the summits all the time," Mayor Baxter said, "and the news always draws attention from you Albany guys. You like to drive up here and gawk at the locals, don't you?"

Fred laughed when the mayor got his jab in.

"Don't be ridiculous," the mayor continued. "Them campers likely wandered off the marked paths or traveled up the peak without signing in at the trailhead. Dangerous, but people do that sometimes. Don't you worry though, our local boys know these mountains. We'll find 'em. Besides…" the mayor smiled and paused for effect. Something Fred had seen him do a ton of times. "Bigfoot is good people. Friendly. And you can quote me on that. Be sure to stick around for the festivities, ya hear?"

"So, you think they're lost? Second time in two days people went missing." Another reporter called out.

The mayor pulled a cigar out of his front shirt pocket and a lighter from his jeans. He flicked the top open and puffed the cigar until the tip lit up red. He glared at the out-of-towner but didn't respond.

"My sources said their car was abandoned on the roadside." The reporter opened a small notepad. "A blue '96 Honda Civic. And the couple is not answering their cellphones."

Mayor Baxter smiled and wagged a finger. "The cell towers don't reach most our mountains. Hikers usually got no service. Not answering cell calls is no cause for alarm. And cars parked next to the trailheads ain't considered abandoned after one night. Where do you expect folks to park, top of a mountain peak?"

Then the mayor laughed, hard and loud. But the hair on Fred's neck stood on end. He remembered the blue car from the night before and hoped the snow-globe-shaking couple didn't go up the summits unprepared.

"How do you explain the last campsite? 'Ravaged by a wild animal,' the police report says."

Alarmed murmurs came from the onlookers who, until that moment, were watching quietly.

"The official report," Mayor Baxter said, "has not been released yet. So, I don't know how reliable your 'source' is—"

"It's reliable."

Baxter tossed his barely smoked cigar into the street. "Them campers were inexperienced. Left fire burning and food unattended. Attracts all kinds of wildlife."

The reporter uncapped a pen and scribbled in the book. "So, your official story is the campers are lost, but nothing bad has happened to them. Right. Any comment on the YouTube footage released?"

Fred cringed. That was the first time Granddad moved, and visible pupils or not, Fred was certain his eyes shifted in his direction. After adding the latest evidence to his presentation, he'd uploaded the footage. But as of that morning, the new vid on his channel had only a few views.

The mayor stared at the reporter for a moment and adjusted his ball cap. "You have my comments." He turned his back on the crowd and walked into the building.

As the people dispersed, Fred caught sight of an unmistakable shock of blonde curls. "Cindy, wait."

He stomped on the back of his board, tucked it beneath his arm, and sprinted to catch up. Cindy rounded the corner, and Fred ran into a trio of Lacrosse Losers.

"Where ya going, Nerd-brain?"

Luke Meriwether stood a head taller than Fred, an intimidating fool who delighted in picking on anyone smaller than him. The milk-pale, freckled face lacrosse captain made him nauseous.

If Cindy wasn't watching, he'd sock Luke right in the lip. Maybe his mouth would blow up and stop him from speaking. But in return, Luke would pound him until his eyes swelled shut. Fred's narrow shoulders and skinny arms would be no match. Besides, he didn't use his fists. He flexed his cranium muscle, something Luke could not do because it required an actual brain.

"Figures you'd be at Baxter's ridiculous Bigfoot news conference. You and that idiot got a lot in common."

Jeers erupted from Meriwether's two minions, Jesse and Tom. The Baker cousins were an amusing pair. Jesse was lanky and making waves on the team. What Tom lacked in muscle, he made up for in smiles, with a stupid permanent grin fixed on his thin face.

"Out of the way, Luke." Fred glanced sideways and pushed his glasses higher on the bridge of his nose. Cindy chewed her lip. She did that when she was nervous. Then she turned and walked away.

Luke shouted to his teammates coming up the block. "Hey, guys, look! Moody still believes in Bigfoot. How pathetic is that?"

The jocks laughed.

A vein throbbed in Fred's neck. Those guys were such jerks. He shouldered past Luke. "I need to get to class. Some of us have a future that doesn't involve playing with a ball and a stick."

"Oh, snap!" Jesse Baker said. "Dude, you gonna let him talk to you like that?"

Fred hopped on his skateboard and headed toward the school.

"Too many people around," Luke said, followed by something Fred couldn't make out but made the guys laugh again.

He had to put those losers out of his mind. He had his proof. And once he showed it, no one would laugh at him anymore.

# THREE

## Fourth Period Global Studies

M s. Ryan sat back in her old wooden chair, looking completely out of place with her long dark hair, crystal hanging around her neck, and warm smile. "Mr. Moody, you're next," she said.

Fred practically jumped to his feet, and the entire class groaned.

He made his way to the front of the classroom with a stack of papers, an iPad, and his night-vision goggles. He dropped the mess in a heap on the teacher's desk, pushed a stray curl out of his eye, and fished around for the remote clicker in the pile.

"Freaking Einstein," a boy's voice came from the back of the room.

Fred glared at the crapweasel. He ignored Luke and his stupid friends. This was his chance. He'd prepared all summer, practiced in the mirror, even gathered old newspapers from the early twentieth century. He had only to convince Cindy he wasn't crazy. Then she'd forgive him, and everything would go back to normal. And he wouldn't let Luke mess it up.

"Get on with it, Einstein," Liza said. "We'd all like to head off to snoozeville."

Liza Jordan, Cindy's new best friend.

He drew air in through his nose and held it a few seconds, so he wasn't tempted to bounce his red laser pointer off her shiny forehead. He'd put up with the pony-tailed kleptomaniac helping herself to his stuff in math class all last year. Liza was why he started attaching tracker tags to his things. Plus, she'd stolen his best friend and started the whole "Einstein" thing. His face flushed hotly just thinking about it.

It was his fourth-grade science project—quantum entanglement—Einstein's theory of spooky movement at a distance, that had earned him the annoying nickname. The project was awesome, but all anyone remembered was Liza commenting on his hair sticking up just like Einstein's. Even his teachers had adopted the name.

"That's enough," Ms. Ryan said. "We will respect our classmates."

"Can you turn the lights off please?" Fred asked.

Ms. Ryan nodded to Parker Thomas, whose desk was closest to the switch. Most of the class sat in a semi-circle, or just squatted on the floor. The troublemakers—like Luke and his minions—clung to the back of the room. Ms. Ryan liked to keep what she called an informal learning environment, but sometimes it felt more like a three-ring circus. Cindy and Liza lounged on twin beanbag chairs—front and center. No pressure. He slipped the night-goggles on his head.

Parker made a face and then flicked the room into darkness, allowing Fred's opening slide to come into focus. White letters on a black background: Giants of North America.

The groans got louder.

"This is the same project he did last year!" Parker shouted.

"Oh no," Liza's nasty voice interrupted. "Not exactly. This year he's wearing some kind of space glasses on his head."

"They're not space glasses, dummy." Fred clicked his remote, and the words, *A Conspiracy to Snub History*, appeared as a subtitle. And he began, "As many of you know—"

"Yeah, everyone knows from last year, and the one before that," Liza said.

Fred ignored her. "This history is about stories. And it's the same story told throughout time and across cultures. And set in stone all over the world." He clicked to the next slide: "Anasazi petroglyphs wall, Utah." It showed a picture of drawings on ruined rocks that looked as if scribbled on by kids with sidewalk chalk.

He moved through several more slides with walls full of chalk figures. "See these footprints the natives drew side-by-side?"

A close-up of chalk feet.

"The larger sets have six toes, like in giant lore and the biblical Nephilim. The smaller, human ones have five toes."

Another click.

"And these..." Fred said, pointing to a picture of the handprints. "Same thing. Six fingers on giant hands. Five on human hands."

"That doesn't prove anything, dweeb," Luke yelled.

Ms. Ryan's lips pressed into a tight line, and she held up a hand. "Enough, Mr. Meriwether. One more outburst, and you'll be sitting in Principal Marsh's office. Continue, Frederick. This project is very interesting."

"Yeah, because she didn't hear it last year." Luke's goon squad hooted and high-fived him.

"Out, boys." Ms. Ryan pointed to the door. "Now."

The three jocks in their stupid, matching red-and-white school lacrosse jackets shuffled toward the door. "At least we got out of listening to Einstein's conspiracy craziness," Luke said as he left.

Fred took a deep breath and pressed on. "All cultures, all the way back to the cavemen, carved pictures and told stories of gigantic, fur-covered men living in the forests."

"Those are only stories—Bigfoot is not real," Parker said, rolling his eyes.

Fred glared at him. "Giants are real. And Bigfoots are a type of giant."

The next slides showed pictures from the previous year's festival with banners featuring hairy North American Sasquatches and Himalayan Yetis. "People from all around the world have reported giant sightings," Fred said.

Click.

"Quotes from Enochian texts described fallen angels creating giants. Images of Thor, Hercules, Skunny-Wundy, and David fighting Goliath. Scottish berserkers and the Irish giant, Fionn Mac Cumhaill. There are tons of giant legends in many cultures. Even popular fictional stories, like vampires, have their roots in giant lore. Some giants were cannibals and drank blood. That's where vampire stories came from."

Fred clicked through a series of giant statues and rock formations. "Legends say that the sun petrifies giants and turns them to stone. And as you can see, these mysterious formations popped up all over the world."

Liza leaned back in the beanbag chair and crossed her arm. "So, what's with the space goggles, Einstein?"

She was so annoying. Fred wasn't sure who was worse, her, or Luke. He wiped his sweaty palms on his pants. "Infrared night-vision camera goggles. You know, for taking video in the dark."

He moved on, clicking through slides showing pictures of his dad at the Ohio mounds, newspaper clippings of giant remains found outside Watertown, and of Fred wearing a wide Kool-Aid smile in front of the Smithsonian Institute in Washington, D.C.

"What most people consider stories, scientists and bio-archeologists, like my dad, take seriously. Many newspapers in the early twentieth century reported excavated gigantic human bones, which were sent to the Smithsonian."

He clicked the slide one more time. His favorite picture of him and his parents standing next to Dr. Joplin in D.C. "But," Fred said, "the most organizationally detailed agency in the world admitted to mysteriously losing the bones without explanation."

Fred allowed those words to sink in for a moment.

"Egyptian hieroglyphics showed giant men standing next to much smaller men. And everywhere pyramids appear on Earth mark places where giants were spotted throughout history."

"History?" Ms. Ryan interrupted. "You mean mythology."

"No, ma'am. History. Amerigo Vespucci, the explorer and cartographer, recorded giants in his explorations when he landed in South America. As did Magellan, Columbus, Lewis and Clarke... But the accounts were scrubbed from the history books—written off as unreliable. How could Vespucci be credible enough to map the New World, but not trustworthy enough to report what he saw there? That doesn't make any sense."

Ms. Ryan raised an eyebrow. "Go on."

"The same thing happened with ancient and biblical texts. Way back when the Catholic Church decided what books would stay in the Bible, Constantine declared certain books, like the Book of Jubilees, Enoch, and the Apocalypse of Abraham, stricken from biblical canon. Dead Sea Scrolls proved these books were all part of the original Jewish Torah. But after maintaining their place for over 2,000 years, they were removed. Do you know what all the books have in common? They all reference the existence of giants in their texts."

Fred wiped his palms again and stole a glance at Cindy. Her head was flopped forward, face buried in her hands. He sighed and looked around the classroom. Aiden was fast asleep. Robert had his textbook open, and Taylor was reading a book about raising horses. He needed to speed things up—get to the good part.

The next slide showed a picture of his parents standing in a pile of gigantic bones.

"Ew!" Molly squealed.

"All right," Ms. Ryan said. "Let's move along. Time is almost up. Explain what you have here." She motioned to the pile on her desk.

Fred grabbed the iPad, pulled up his YouTube channel, and turned the screen toward the class. "The infrared night cameras recorded movement in the forest last night."

The video, awash with a green glow, played strange howling and knocking sounds. "Right here." Fred pointed to the upper left side of the screen. Tree limbs shook as if a strong wind had blown through, but only in one small patch of forest. Branches snapped with a rhythmic crunching. "Something was out there."

"So what?" Liza, again.

"Don't you ever raise your hand?" Fred wondered why Ms. Ryan never threw Liza out of the room.

"Einstein, why does it matter? They're all dead skeletons."

Fred pushed his glasses higher on the bridge of his nose. The back of his neck prickled beneath his collar. "It matters because they are not all gone. Some are still here, like Bigfoots."

Liza sat real straight and waved her hand in the air. Then without even being called on, she said, "You mean Bigfeet."

Cindy raised her head and said half-heartedly. "No, it's Bigfoots." Her eyes got all wide like she'd just realized she said the words out loud.

The klepto's face turned all red, and she glared at Cindy.

Fred couldn't help but smile. "Someone is systematically hiding aspects of human history. And they've been doing it for hundreds of years," he said.

Parker leaned on the wall next to the light switch with both hands in his front jean pockets. "Why would anyone do that?"

"So no one would believe they exist," Fred said.

"Because they don't," Liza said.

And that was Fred's cue—the one he'd waited for. Time for the big reveal. A bead of sweat rolled down the back of his neck. He clicked on his final slide and smiled so wide he thought his face would split in half. "Then, what is this?"

On the screen, a close-up of a giant muddy footprint appeared. "I found this print at the missing camper's site last night."

Cindy's head snapped up. "You what?"

"I followed the officers and hid in the tree line. When they left, I did some investigating of my own and found it a few feet away. It has to be related."

Cindy stared at Fred, her honey-blonde hair back in a loose braid, a few wavelets pouring out around her face. Her lips pulled up slightly at the ends.

*I did it! Cindy believes me.*

This time Liza didn't bother raising her hand. "That footprint has five toes. You said giants have six."

Fred narrowed his eyes. He wanted to toss his goggles at her head. Instead, he walked to the projection screen and counted the five clear toes. He pointed to where the sixth should've been. "The print was smeared, but if you look at the depression here, that is clearly toe number six."

"It's a big smudge," Parker protested.

"Mr. Moody," Ms. Ryan said. "That's not funny. Going into the woods and making up stories about giant footprints while police are looking for missing campers is going too far."

Before Fred could defend himself, the bell rang. But he hadn't made anything up! He looked to Cindy, but she was already following Liza out the door.

Fine.

He would prove it. Keep searching. Set up more equipment. Find Bigfoot. He'd show them giants exist. Get proof. Real. Live. Proof. He had to. Then his grandfather and his teachers would believe him, his parents would come home, and Luke and his henchmen would lay off.

But most importantly, everything would return to normal with Cindy. He'd prove it. Get his friend back. Whatever it took.

# FOUR

## Thursday – Sixth Period

L UNCH TOTALLY SUCKED.

The cafeteria at Village Middle was larger than one would expect, and with kids from the older grades, not the friendliest of places. The "middle-school" occupied the second floor of the building, sandwiched between the elementary on the third, and the high-schoolers on the first. But in elementary, they had the lunchroom to themselves. Now they shared it with the upper grades.

Fred lingered at the end of the food line, pondering how to find a real live Bigfoot. He knew it was out there, had tons of evidence. But without the creature itself, his mission was hopeless. He stared at his tray: sloppy joe, nacho chips, an apple, cold baked beans, half-thawed fruit cup, and warm milk. Ugh. Then he spotted Cindy.

She was sitting alone at a table across the room, swirling a fork around in the beans. Fred waved, and her mouth spread into a broad smile. It made her eyes scrunch and crinkled the light dusting of freckles on her cheeks. He started toward her, the day finally looking up.

Then Liza sat. She was saying something that he couldn't decipher over all the noise in the cafeteria, but Cindy suddenly set her fork next to the milk container, and her whole expression changed. Lips pressed together and cheeks turned pink. She blinked a few times, and it seemed as if her big almond eyes shined. It reminded Fred of the expression she got when being scolded in public. Her mom yelled a lot.

Usually, Fred would've veered right or left and slid into a chair at another table. But not that day. That day, something inside him puffed up. He wouldn't let Liza stop him. He glared at her streaked brown hair jerking from side to side, strode right up behind her and sat on the end of the cafeteria bench, nudging Liza's tray with his own.

Fred smiled. "Hey, Cynd."

Liza's nose scrunched as if she'd stuck it in a trash heap. "What are you doing here, Einstein?"

Fred ignored her. "Going to the festival tomorrow night?"

Cindy nodded. "Everyone is."

"Not me," Liza said.

"What? I thought we were picking you up," Cindy said.

Liza shrugged. "Mom's dragging me to Plattsburgh. I won't miss much."

"Only the band, parade, and all the lacrosse guys manning the games and food booths," Cindy said.

"She promised to drop me at your place on Saturday morning."

Liza lived out on Hwy 86 in the middle of nowhere. Took 35 minutes by car just to get into town. Since Cindy had moved out of the house next door to Fred, she only needed to walk downstairs and step onto Main Street to be in the middle of the festivities. Cindy's apartment was three blocks from Fred's house, but felt farther than driving halfway to

Albany. He tried not to think about that and focused on what Liza had said. She would not be at the festival on Friday night.

"I heard Coach Bender volunteered Luke for the dunking tank," Cindy said.

The girls laughed.

Fred beamed. Things were getting better and better. "I still have our costumes from last year," he said. "I mean, they might be a little tight—and short—but we haven't grown that much."

"What are you trying to say, Einstein? Cindy didn't gain *that* much weight over the summer."

"No... I didn't mean. Wait. What? No—"

Cindy turned the color of the apple sitting on Fred's plate, a sort of purplish-red, and pushed her tray away.

Liza rolled her eyes. "Besides, costumes are so fifth grade." She stood and motioned for Cindy to follow. "I've energy bars in my locker. I'm not eating this garbage."

Fred lifted his chin and took a bite. The "joe" slopped over the side of the bun, ran down his hands, and dripped on the tray. It tasted like greasy meat soup on mush bread, but he didn't care. Liza thought she was better than everyone else was. Too good for lunchroom food.

Cindy handed Fred a napkin, glanced sideways and whispered, "Did you really find that footprint at the camp?"

Liza scowled and shot Cindy a look.

The thought of the ravished site sent a shiver crawling up Fred's arms like a wave of ants. "Yeah, I could show you where—"

Liza crossed her arms. "Seriously? You've been harping on this giant thing since the second grade. Nobody cares."

"Nobody is talking to you." Fred put the sloppy sandwich back on his tray and wiped his greasy fingers on the napkin.

Liza tossed her book bag over her shoulder and headed toward the lockers lining the right side of the cafeteria.

Cindy stood, looking uncertain.

"I could show you after school."

She chewed her lip. "Um... maybe... I—"

"Great! Meet me at Baker's Head."

"You coming or what?" Liza called from across the room.

"Yeah, okay," Cindy said and hurried after the friend-stealing snot face.

"Cindy," Fred called. "Don't go through the woods, okay?"

*"Don't go through the woods,"* a mocking voice said close to his ear. "When you gonna get it, Moody? She doesn't want to hang out with you anymore. You're too much of a dweeb." Luke snatched the night-vision camera goggles off Fred's head. He hadn't realized he was still wearing them.

"I'll take these. Come on, guys," Luke called to his friends. "Maybe I'll see Bigfoot when I climb the *Drop.*"

Deadman's Drop, or the *"Drop,"* is the highest, most dangerous climb in the six mountains surrounding the village of Six Summit Lake. Luke was such a blowhole. Granddad said no one could climb the *Drop.*

Luke slipped the goggles onto his face. "Hey, look at me. I'm nerd-brain Moody."

The lacrosse guys laughed. So did Parker and Molly sitting at a nearby table.

"Stop being a jerk, Luke," Fred shouted, except he didn't say *jerk.* He used another word that was way more accurate. But even the crapweasel couldn't dampen his mood. He wasn't even mad about his goggles. He had a back-up pair. All that mattered right then was showing Cindy proof.

Only—Coach Bender turned around exactly when Fred called Luke the word that was not *jerk*.

"Moody, let's go." The squat lacrosse coach motioned for Fred to follow.

When Bender turned his back, Luke snatched the apple from Fred's tray and launched it at Bender's head. The fruit found its target and bounced off his shiny bald spot.

The lunchroom erupted in laughter.

Bender spun, his face devil-red. Burning coal eyes homed in on Fred.

Luke's mop of straight brown hair flopped across one of his eyes when he smiled.

"Move it, kid," Bender said. He pushed through the cafeteria doors just as the bell rang and the hallway flooded with students. Luke's gang walked in the opposite direction, nudging unsuspecting fifth graders out of the way, sending them careening into the lockers. A chorus of laughter followed a lame joke Coach Bender didn't seem to hear. Although for a moment, Fred thought a smirk appeared on the teacher's face.

Fred padded down the steps to the dean's office.

Great. Another afternoon of mind-numbing detention. Pointing out that Meriwether was responsible had been hopeless. In Bender's eyes, Luke never stepped out of line. He was the team's star player, and the coach was pining for another trophy.

Fred tried to catch up with Cindy in the hallways to tell her he'd gotten detention, but she rushed out of their classes. And by the time he got out of school, the trails were empty.

He jogged the winding path, pushing aside tangles of branches. The forest floor crinkled. Sweat rolled down his face. Sunlight arrowed through the canopy, but the air was cooler among the trees. A squirrel scurried in front of his feet. When he reached Baker's Trailhead, his lungs deflated and felt as if they'd stuck to the back of his ribs. Cindy was not there.

It was all Luke's fault. The jerk ruined everything.

Fred considered walking over to Cindy's apartment, but if Liza was there, it would be pointless. Besides, he intended to head out after dark in search of more evidence. Maybe even find the creature and show the whole town at the festival.

Thinking about the festival made him feel better. No Liza, at least for one night. But of all the kids he hoped wouldn't show, Luke Meriwether made the top of the list.

# FIVE

## Friday

FRED HAD FOURTEEN TRAP cameras set up within a two-mile radius of his house. They were motion activated and would snap pictures of anything that triggered them. Over the summer, Cindy questioned whether Bigfoot would come that close to town. But he reminded her of all the sightings close to villages. It seemed as if the creatures got curious about humans, venturing into campsites and backyards. Some folks even claimed to set out food as a lure.

Purple and streaks of orange peeked over the treetops by the time Fred checked all his equipment and relocated a camera to the scene of the crime, hoping Bigfoot would return to the campsite. He wanted to snap a few more shots of the footprint, but it was gone, washed away like footprints on the beach when the tide comes in. Only he wasn't at the beach, and it hadn't rained.

Fred was adjusting the sights on his back-up goggles when he noticed a movement farther down the trail. He squinted. Whatever moved through the trees was trying hard to be sneaky, and it was working.

Realizing with horror he had left his bow back in the Watchcave, he looked around for something to use as a weapon. He snatched a solid stick from the forest floor and ran down the path. He just needed to capture some footage. But when he reached the spot, whatever had been there was gone.

Fred spied bushes moving. He was off again, dashing up the incline, the woods awash in an eerie green glow. A knocking as if someone was banging on a hollowed-out tree trunk, only a gazillion times louder, echoed through the woods. He fixed his eyes on the moving undergrowth ahead and sprinted, ducking beneath branches and bounding through bushes. He leaped over roots and rocks, confident he was chasing a giant.

Branches and leaves rustled just ahead of him. A dark shape darted to the left, trying to veer away from the path, grunting. Fred's heart raced. Bigfoot was out there. He changed the angle of his sprint and dove left to cut it off. He exploded through the undergrowth, Go-Pro attached to his goggles, recording.

Nothing. What the—? Where did it go?

He spun in a circle, scanning the tree line. The knocking stopped. The air was still and the woods quiet, but energy like an electrical current zipped up and down Fred's legs. His hands shook, and his pulse raced. He'd seen the creature.

Okay, he'd seen a large, dark, beast-like shape. He snatched the camera from its mount on his headgear and reviewed the footage. "Yes," he yelled aloud. His Go-Pro had picked up the creature.

It weaved in and out of the trees, shaking bushes and snapping branches as it went. The video was dark and fuzzy, but still, no one could deny something was out there.

"There's nothing out there in them woods." Granddad's brow scrunched together. "All that film shows is a fuzzy outline. Could easily be someone messing about in one of them costumes. Now shut it down and get some sleep."

Fred's eyes burned. "Can't," he said. "Got school."

Granddad had found out about the footprint and his snooping and his sneaking out to find Bigfoot. And when Fred crept into the Watchcave just past six, he'd been waiting. The only effect showing him the pictures and video footage had was to lengthen the lecture. He would've almost preferred a grounding—if it weren't festival weekend.

Fred rested his head on the computer desk for only a moment, then awoke in a puddle of his own drool. A note from his granddad lay next to the keyboard, instructing him to come to the town hall when he woke. He wiped away a sticky string of saliva and checked his watch. Holy eight pm! He'd slept all day.

He slipped on his skate shoes, grabbed his board, a bow, a quiver full of arrows, and headed for the door without changing his jeans or the two-day-old rumpled Fortnite shirt. He didn't even bother with a sniff test.

On his way down the driveway, Aunt Faye warned him to behave and leave his inventions home. She didn't want a repeat of the disaster the year before when he'd tried to show Cindy how his rapid-launching boomerang arrows worked. Unfortunately, the bolt had chased Jesse Baker around the auditorium, and then flew through a 100-year-old stained-glass window. Granddad forbade him to test any of his inventions inside buildings for the foreseeable future.

Fred had made significant adjustments since then to avoid any such mishap, but he did as he was told. He didn't bring the boomerang arrow launcher inside the hall. He stashed it behind the building in a big bush next to the riverbank. Just in case.

Fred stood at the entrance of the hall with one foot on the first step. He wasn't looking forward to going inside. Why couldn't Granddad give him the long version of the lecture after the festival? Cindy had a 9 o'clock curfew, so he probably wouldn't get to talk to her. He'd still be getting lectured by the time she needed to be home, which was totally unfair. He backed down the step. Maybe he could find her real quick. Five more minutes wouldn't hurt.

Fred moved through the crush of people milling around the sawdust-covered paths. The fair celebrated Bigfoot, but was just as much about fried dough, funnel cakes, cotton candy, and deep-fried Oreos. And the lacrosse team had their hands full manning the ring toss and the dime pitch. Fred looked for the ping pong ball in the fishbowl game even though the prize died by the time the winner got home.

Everyone walked in groups or at least pairs, laughing and joking as they waded through crowds and carnival games, or stood in line to buy tickets to rides.

He spotted Cindy standing alone in the popcorn line. Her blonde hair fell in ringlets over her shoulders, and she wore her book bag backward. An orange and white striped furry cat head stuck out of the top. Tiger.

Tiger was a stray until that February day in the fifth grade when Fred tested his snowball pitcher. It worked a little too well. Took out two of Mrs. Kearney's windows, which cost Fred six months allowance. Unluckily, the cat strolled across the street just as he lunged to shut his invention down. The snowball pitcher tipped over and pitched an ice ball, hitting Tiger in his hind leg. It wasn't broken, but Cindy didn't know it at the time. She splinted the leg and carried the poor thing on a homemade stretcher.

Cindy always loved cats. She volunteered at the Humane Society every Saturday just to play with them. Fred hadn't seen Tiger in forever. Then he remembered, Liza was allergic to cats. And it was a Liza-free night.

Fred stepped around a couple in matching Bigfoot costumes pushing a toddler in a stroller. The small boy clutched a brownish red-haired doll with bright yellow eyes and made a face at Fred. All these people, the visitors and town folk, came out to celebrate and claim they believed—but they didn't.

Folk music blared from the bandstand, and the bonfire in the center of the green roared and crackled. "Cindy," Fred called, but she didn't turn around. He wound through the crowd, past the Ferris wheel, Tilt-a-Whirl, and the teacup ride. By the time he got to the popcorn line, she was gone.

Fred jumped at the boom of the first fireworks lighting up the sky in a burst of color. Nine o'clock. He sighed. *Let's get this over with.*

Granddad's office was usually a quiet place, even during festival time. So, when Fred stepped through the door, he didn't expect a room filled with people. He stood on his tip toes to look over the head of someone he didn't recognize, but didn't find his granddad anywhere.

Murmurs about a boy and the woods filled the space as Fred pushed through the crowd. Granddad stood in Mayor Baxter's office with the door closed. The office was like a fishbowl. Glass walls and a glass door—part of Baxter's transparency campaign. Granddad's back was to the hallway. His arms waved around in the air like they do when he's angry. Whatever his granddad said must have upset the mayor, too, because his face was the red-purple shade of Aunt Faye's beets.

All eyes watched as if they were visiting an aquarium, fascinated by a surprise confrontation between a great whale and a killer shark who should've never been placed in the same tank. Although Fred wasn't sure who was the whale and who was the shark at that moment.

His granddad turned from the mayor's desk and flung the glass door open. "We'll search the summits ourselves," he said. "I'm not waiting for the state police."

Voices in the room grew louder, and many in the crowd nodded in agreement. So focused on the spectacle, Fred hadn't realized Cindy had slipped into the small space next to him. Not until she elbowed him in the rib. "What's going on?"

"Sounds like a missing hiker." Fred smiled, without taking his eyes off his granddad and the mayor.

"This is my town," the mayor's voice boomed. He came around from behind his desk.

Granddad spun to face him. "And I'm sheriff here!"

"That doesn't have to be the case anymore, does it?"

And for a moment, Fred thought Baxter would actually hit his granddad. He surged toward the door.

Granddad stepped close to Mayor Baxter, and Fred could almost hear the whole room hold its breath. Talking toned down to a low buzz, a few gasps, and then to complete silence. And still, he couldn't make out the exact words his granddad growled. It must've been bad because the mayor turned from the color of beets to the color of parsnip in about a second flat.

Mayor Baxter ran his hand through his thinning silver-blond hair, looking as if he would say something but thought better of it. Granddad stormed through the crowd toward his office. People were yelling a gazillion questions all at once. And when he turned around, everyone went silent again.

"This looks bad," Cindy said.

Fred shook his head but didn't take his eyes off his granddad. He'd never seen such a concerned look on his face.

"Something's not right," Cindy said. "More missing campers?"

Fred doubted what was going on had anything to do with lost campers. People got turned around all the time in the mountains, and his granddad never acted like that. He stayed calm and level-headed. Fred thought of the footprints, dark figure, and weird sounds in the woods. The inside of his stomach knotted into a tangled lump.

Surveying the room, Granddad cleared his throat, and said, "Gather your gear and meet back in ten. We'll fan out in groups and search the summits ourselves. We cannot afford to wait for the state police." He shot a sharp glance at the mayor.

A woman's voice Fred didn't recognize came from somewhere behind him. "Do you think that's safe? I heard blood covered the tents where the last ones went missing like something tore those campers apart."

Everyone talked at once.

"Poppycock," Granddad shouted. "None of that is true. No blood or bodies were found at the campsite, so we don't know what happened. And as for the boy, he's one of our own, and we *will* go find him."

"What does he mean?" Cindy asked.

Fred had nearly forgot she was there. "Let's grab jackets and extra flashlights. It doesn't sound good."

A couple dozen people remained in the room, but they were all on the move, heading toward the exit. "Wait," Fred yelled. "Who's missing?"

Mayor Baxter looked at him as if he'd asked the strangest question ever. Did the crowd know what Granddad would say? Did they know something he didn't? Everyone always knew something Fred didn't.

Granddad seemed to flinch. His eyes were shiny and wet and had a look about them Fred had not seen before. "Luke Meriwether," he said, and without another word, stepped into his office.

# SIX

FRED'S FEET ROOTED TO the floor. Luke? He never thought a classmate would go missing.

"Oh my god, Liza," Cindy said.

Fred groaned. Liza had been crushing on Luke since third grade. Cindy's voice got his body moving.

"Maybe he's just lost," Fred said. "We need to help find him."

Luke was a jerk, but Fred didn't want anything to happen to him. Well, not too much, at least. Freezing his stupid butt off lost in the woods for a few hours would serve him right. He scolded himself for that thought, but only a little.

Fred turned to follow Cindy out of the building, but a firm hand gripped his shoulder. The old man's strength always surprised him.

"Wait, son," Granddad said.

Cindy winced. So did Fred.

"Why don't you and Cynthia meet your friends at the festival?" He pulled two twenty-dollar bills out of his wallet and handed them to Fred. Granddad's way of telling him they weren't coming. "Have a good time."

"We want to help," Fred said. Why did everyone think just because they were kids, they'd be useless to the search party? He knew the mountains better than most people preparing to head out. He wanted to scream.

"It's dark," Granddad said.

"I'll wear night-vision goggles—"

"No. Stay at the festival."

Fred opened his mouth to continue to argue, but his granddad walked away as if there was nothing else to say.

Cindy looked at Fred with those *I'm sorry you're so pathetic even your granddad won't let you go with him* eyes. Fred hated that look. But he had an idea. "Still want to see where I found the print?"

"What are you going to do?"

Fred pushed out the door and stomped down the side steps. Cindy trailed behind. He rounded the building and retrieved his boomerang arrow launcher from the bushes.

Her eyes widened. "Is that—?"

"Don't worry, I've worked out the kinks." He handed her his bow and quiver. "You might need these."

Cindy seemed to clutch her book bag closer, Tiger wiggling inside. She narrowed her eyes, and her mouth opened as if she would say something. Then she pressed her lips in a thin line. Fred thought she'd say she was going home, but she slung the quiver over her shoulder and took the weapon. He couldn't help but smile.

"Come on." Fred slipped the night-vision goggles on his head and turned for the path, hoping the search parties wouldn't take Baker's Trail. He'd head up the summits, find the giant's nest, and track down that idiot Luke—before he got eaten. It shouldn't have, but the thought kind of made Fred chuckle. *Local dumb-head consumed by Bigfoot.*

# SEVEN

## Luke

A KNOCKING SOUND SLOWLY roused Luke to consciousness. The steady *knock knock knock* echoed from somewhere in the distance. His mouth tasted salty and metallic, and a foul stench clogged his nostrils. It was dark and dank, and a large animal splayed across the stone floor in front of him. It lay flat like a bear skin rug.

He closed his eyes, trying to remember how he got there. Bender volunteered them to work the festival, but he and Tom and Jesse ditched. He'd been boasting around the fire, telling them he would climb the *Drop*, but they didn't believe him.

His vision cleared a little, bringing the damp cave into sharper focus. Only moonlight shining through an opening lit the space. His memory was hazy and disjointed. He recalled walking off into the woods to take a whizz...

He tried to push himself off the floor only to realize his hands were bound. Pain shot through his eye and his temples pounded. That explained why he couldn't remember. Someone must've hit him in the head.

Luke struggled once more to rise. He rolled to his elbows and knees. His feet were tied together, too. He flopped back on his side, pressing his back against the rock wall. He felt as if a truck had hit him, repeatedly. Sucking in a raspy breath, he squinted into the shadows, watching for the rise and fall of fur. The thing didn't move. He inched forward and nudged the creature with the toe of his sneaker. Nothing. With his heart rate increasing, he poked the fur again. He was glad nothing moved, but what was it?

His face was wet, and he lifted his shoulder to wipe the stream off his cheek. Even in the dimness of moonlight, he could see the sheen of blood on his ruined T-shirt. It was in his hair, down the side of his face, and still dripping into his eyes.

His brain sputtered to remember small flashes of what had happened... The snort that caused him to look up. A giant shadow. The monstrous sight lurking in the trees. Fur. Teeth.

His head was dizzy.

A heavy thump came suddenly from outside the cave. A shadow grew high on the wall. Luke struggled to make sense of what was happening. Footsteps moved closer. What walked into the cave confirmed Luke's worst nightmares.

He scrambled back away from the light into the recesses of the dark chamber. The panic from the night before multiplied tenfold. The monster approached, its massive form hunching to get into the cavern. Muscles rippled across an enormous chest, and its obsidian eyes stared into his own. Luke remembered the events. Camping. Tom and Jesse chugging cans of cola. Screams. He thought they were acting stupid. Playing a prank. He never thought that nerd-brain Moody could be right.

# EIGHT

"FREDDIE, WAIT." CINDY TUGGED on his arm. "I'm not going into the woods. Let the police handle it. Besides, it's after nine, and my mom will kill me if I don't get home. You know how she is."

Cindy's phone dinged. She showed Fred the text: *Why are you still at Town Hall?*

"See," Cindy said. "She's already tracked my location. I got to go."

"We can't leave that crapweasel out in the woods. Not with Bigfoot running around."

Cindy sighed. "He's probably lost. The search party will find him. I'll come by in the morning. You can show me where you found the print then, okay?"

Fred kicked a rock across the parking lot behind the building, trying to hide his disappointment. "Yeah, okay."

"Don't go into the woods tonight," Cindy said. "Promise."

Fred frowned, but he agreed.

Cindy returned the bow and quiver. "Tomorrow about noon, okay?"

Before Fred answered, Cindy's phone dinged again. She glanced at the screen.

"Your mom?" Fred asked.

"No, Liza found out about Luke. I got to go." Without another word or glance back, Cindy rushed along the sidewalk, eyes on her phone, one hand holding onto Tiger in the book bag across her chest and texting with the other.

He'd tried to keep his promise. He intended to—even walked back down the street through the dispersing festival crowd. But the washed-away footprint nagged at him. Maybe Cindy was right, and the police would find Luke. The jerk could be lost, but Luke couldn't be that stupid. He'd grown up in

Six Summit Lake the same as Fred, so how could he get turned around? No, something else was going on.

Fred glanced down Main Street toward Cindy's apartment. He hated breaking his promises, but this was too important. Footprint vanished. Footage was fuzzy. And though Bigfoot eating Luke would make Fred's life a lot more pleasant, he still stomped up the trail to search for the stupid-head.

He flipped his night-vision goggles to the "on" position, not wanting the flashlight to call attention. Making his way up the trail, he scrambled over rocks and branches. He clambered over a trunk that blocked the path, slipping on the pinecones dotting the ground like spilt trinkets. He knocked against a tall, thin tree.

Wind tousled its leaves. Trees creaked and groaned and swayed. A branch cracked in the distance. Fred ducked behind an oak. To the right, orbs of light from the searchers efforts popped up and down, but then moved farther away. He let out a breath and waited for them to blink out of sight.

He moved fast, squinting and straining to see. Even with night-vision, his visibility was not very good. Woods were all green and dark and hazy. He wound through the trees and neared the campsite where the last people had gone missing. A set of footprints, which weren't present before, cut up the dirt. He inched forward, following the tracks. Could have been from the search parties, or the state police looking for the hiker, if not for the large, shallow ones set in a weirdly even-spaced pattern moving toward the camp. But they weren't clear through the goggles.

He surveyed the woods. And when he was sure no one was around, he took a utility flashlight from his jacket pocket, flipped the oculars off his eyes, and shone the light on the ground. The footprint had five giant toes. He squatted and ran his fingers over the impression. Weird. The compacted dirt was flat and even. No ridges or heavy heel marks like he would've expected. And it wasn't as deep as the last print he'd found.

A few feet ahead, the big prints mixed with two sets of human-sized prints in what appeared to be a scuffle. Other marks were present too, like sneakers and hiking boots. They all combined in a mess of scattered leaves, dirt, and debris where the non-human prints vanished. Beyond, only sneaker prints and what appeared to be drag marks remained. He snapped pictures as best he could while balancing the flashlight and his phone, not using the night camera. The pictures needed to be clear.

He followed the sneakers and dragged dirt a little way. A bead of sweat trickled down the back of his neck. He shined his flashlight in a circle. To his left, next to a giant oak, he found another set of Bigfoot prints. They were deeper than the giant prints involved in the scuffle and twice as wide. Whatever creature made those prints weighed way more than what made the others. And had six toes. Fred snapped a picture, the light flashing up the tree.

Something dark hung on the tree above his head, and he homed in on its direction. At first, he thought it was a bird, but it didn't move. Snagged on a piece of rough bark was a tuft of black-brown hair about 3 inches long and 2 inches wide, confirming whatever had made those six-toed indentations was tall and furry. He plucked the evidence from the knot, baffled to find the fur silky. He sniffed and regretted it instantly. *Ugh.* Same gross smell as at the campsite the other night.

He slipped the tuft of hair into his evidence bag, a.k.a Aunt Faye's airtight freezer bag, and moved forward, trying to follow the jumble of confusing tracks. They ended near the edge of an embankment. He peered over the side but saw only darkness.

Resting on a rock, Fred set his head in his hands. He stared at the prints nearing the edge. Something small and white mixed with the leaves. He scrambled to the ground, pushing the dirt and the debris aside. A shred of white faux leather.

Fred turned the evidence over in his hands, and a solid lump of clay formed in his throat. He remembered the torn jackets at the campsite, but this patch of material didn't come from those. It looked suspiciously like a piece of lacrosse jacket sleeve. Luke's sleeve. Fred swallowed and glanced toward the ridge. Meriwether might've gone over the side. He shook his head. No. There had to be another explanation. Only he couldn't think of one.

Fred had seen the creature, he was sure of it. Found its hair and part of Luke's jacket. That's when he came to the only conclusion that made any sense: Bigfoot had kidnapped Luke.

Fred dialed Granddad's number and left a long message, telling him everything until the beep cut him off. He closed his fingers around the small piece of material. With that evidence, Granddad would listen. He'd search for the creature, find its nest, and locate Luke before it was too late. He hurried back toward town, eager to take the evidence home. Only one stop to make on the way.

The pebbles knocked against the window, then rained on Fred's head. He lifted a larger rock and chucked it. The stone ricocheted off the sill, landing somewhere in the dimly lit parking lot. "Come on. Wake up. Wake up."

Thankfully, Cindy's bedroom faced the back of the buildings lining Main Street. He could stay out of sight and not get in trouble for attempting to break a window. It wasn't his fault she lived on the third floor. He needed heavy rocks to toss them that high.

He chucked another. A light went on. Blinds split and slid upward. Cindy appeared on the other side of the glass, eyes squinting, and lips pursed. Fred waved.

She opened the window and leaned out. "What are you *doing*?"

"Come down," Fred said, bouncing on his toes.

"It's after midnight. And my mom will be home any minute."

Cindy's mother worked as a nurse out at the old people's home on Highway 9. And always came home grumpy after a 12-hour shift.

"It's important," he said.

"Who's that?" Liza stuck her ugly face out next to Cindy's. Her hair looked like a tangled bird's nest, and her eyes swollen and puffy with sleep. "Einstein?"

Fred groaned. Great. He couldn't be rid of Liza for one night. "I found... Well, clues," he said.

Liza turned from the window.

"Bigfoot kidnapped Luke," he blurted without meaning to, and that made Liza's head snap around.

"You got to be kidding," she said.

"I found footprints in the ground all mixed and tangled like there was a struggle." He pulled the tuft of hair and material from his pocket. "Fur, and well..." He held out the piece of white leather. "This um... Could be part of Luke's jacket."

Liza let out a little yelp and covered her mouth with her hands. But Cindy's face turned serious. "You promised you wouldn't go out into the woods."

"I know, but—"

"What if you tainted the evidence?"

Liza no longer held her mouth. "Or," she said, "maybe he's stealing it. To take the focus off himself. Everyone knows you pick on Luke."

Fred choked on his words. "I pick on *him?*"

But Liza just kept on speaking. "You were the last one to argue with him. If someone kidnapped Luke, you're the number one prime suspect."

"Number one and prime are the same thing, dummy," he said. "And I didn't do anything to Luke. That's ridiculous."

"Why are you removing stuff from the scene? So no one can find him?"

He hated to admit the snot face had a point. What if he was a suspect? Taking the evidence might not have been the best idea, but he couldn't do nothing or leave his discovery in the woods.

"Bring it to your granddad," Cindy said.

"I called him. But you need to see this first."

Liza sniffled as if she was crying or something. Likely a cold from the turning weather. "I'm going back to bed."

"Come down. Just for a minute, please. "Fred pleaded.

But Cindy shook her head. "Go home, Freddie." Then she closed the window and shut the blinds, leaving Fred standing in the dark, feeling stupid.

# NINE

TEN MINUTES LATER, FRED pounded up the stone walk to the front door. The sheriff's cruiser sat in the driveway. "Granddad," he called, closing the heavy wooden door behind him. "You home?" Silence. He shrugged and pulled off his hoodie, dropping it on the floor in the foyer, and was halfway down the hall toward the Watchcave when a door opened behind him.

"Hold it right there, Frederick," Aunt Faye said, sticking her head out of the kitchen. "Where do you think you're going?"

Fred felt the panic flush across his face and rushed back to the foyer, snatching the hoodie from the floor. "I'll put my hoodie in the hamper."

Her dark eyes settled on him. "What time is it?"

"About midnight," Fred said, offering a weak smile. "Thought you'd be sleeping."

"Perhaps I would be, if your granddaddy weren't in here harping about your insubordination and disobedience."

"Aunt Faye," Fred said. "I left him a message so he wouldn't worry."

"A message?" she said. "Something about trampling around in the woods and messing with evidence? What do you have to say for yourself?"

Fred shifted. "Did they find Luke?"

She sighed. "Why do you suppose your granddaddy did not want you in the woods?"

He studied the scuff marks in the hardwood floor while Aunt Faye waited. "Because it's late."

"And?" she said.

Fred winced. "Dangerous."

"You could have got lost. Or been killed," she said, her voice rising to the pitch of a dog whistle. "Heaven knows what wild animal is running amuck."

"Bigfoot kidnapped Luke," he blurted out for the second time that night, and it didn't go over any better. "I tried to find him."

"Other people are working on that. Adults."

"Yeah, but," he said, holding his phone out. "They don't have these pictures of the footprints and—"

Faye held up her hand. "Not another word, Frederick. Your granddaddy is waiting in the garage. Now go. Better not keep him waiting any longer."

*Oh man.* Granddad was in his Watchcave.

"Frederick Albert Moody. What were you doing at my crime scene?"

Fred smoothed his shirt and pulled the stinky patch of fur from his pocket. "Investigating," Fred said, trying to keep his voice professional. Granddad appreciated professionalism. He pushed the evidence toward him. "Fur from the Bigfoot."

Granddad grabbed the tuft. "What the...?"

"And a piece of Luke's jacket. If we can find the creature—did you say *crime* scene? I knew it!"

Fred showed him the pictures. Faux leather lay on top of the desk. The fur stunk up the Watchcave in a mix of burnt wood, smoke, and sweat. He thought he caught a hint of pine needles, but he couldn't be sure.

Granddad just stood there. The evidence to break the case wide open sitting in front of him and he didn't even flinch. Nothing.

"Frederick," he said, without making eye contact. "You're grounded."

"Grounded? For how long?"

"'Til I see fit," he said, snatching the power strip cord from the wall. "And no infonet. You'll do chores around here. You can start at first light."

Granddad did not understand how the internet worked.

"Clean the shed out back."

"The shed?" Fred said. "I thought you'd make me take out the trash or mow the lawn. No one uses the shed."

"Organize the workbench, sweep out the dirt, and broom the cobwebs off the ceiling."

Fred shivered. Spiders. Dark tight places. Not his favorite environments. Okay, maybe he was a little terrified of confined spaces. Not the point. The shed was a dark death trap that almost killed him once already. Aunt Faye wouldn't step foot in the decrepit building on account the shed was liable to fall down around her.

"Granddad, Cindy and I got plans. She's coming over in the morning so we can look over the evidence and see if we can figure out where Bigfoot took Luke." Fred pulled the old article from beneath his keyboard. "It doesn't say where you spotted Bigfoot. If you could tell us, or check the location—"

"Them newspapers don't know squat," Granddad said, raising his voice. "I ain't seen no creature back then, and there's no creature now. If that boy was disappeared, you can be sure it's a flesh-and-blood person who's done it. And you stay away from them woods, you hear? You're lucky you're not in cuffs. Messing with a crime scene is a serious charge."

"No one put up crime scene tape," Fred said. "So, my find was perfectly legal."

"Well, Baxter's party found the site and says there's nothing to be seen. I suspect that's because you took all the evidence."

"What about the fur?"

Granddad sniffed the tuft again and scrunched his nose. He pulled the hairs apart and turned the piece over. "Synthetic. Likely part of a costume some fool been running around inside."

Costume? Fred shook his head and protested, but Granddad's next question stopped him dead.

"What were you and Meriwether arguing about at school? Jesse Baker said he spied a boy poking round in them woods right before Luke gone missing. Dark curly hair and a miner's hat. Sound like anyone you reckon, Frederick?"

Gooseflesh broke out across Fred's arm. Oh gosh! What if Liza was right, and he was a suspect? If Bigfoot ate Luke, he'd go down for it. He shivered. "I didn't do anything to Luke."

"I ain't saying you did. But you can't be messing about while we investigate."

"I wasn't messing about. I found evidence," Fred said, plopping into a vinyl folding chair resting against his chalk wall. "You going to send the fur to the lab?"

"Might not be evidence of anything." Granddad ran his hand through his hair. "Still, I suppose I can't ignore it either." He scooped up the pieces of leather and fur. "Joe will bag these for the lab."

Fred smiled and sat forward on the chair. "So, what's your take on what happened? One investigator to another?"

"You're not an investigator."

"Well, then, as a kidnapping suspect, I've a right to know."

"No one said nothing about no kidnapping either." Granddad glanced at the Watchcave wall covered in photos and clippings. "Now get up to bed. I want you up with the chickens and working in the shed first thing. I'll check on you when I get home. And I don't want to listen to no more of this Bigfoot nonsense."

# TEN

FRED TRUDGED ACROSS THE knee-deep grass behind the house, horrified, staring at the old shed. It was tall and windowless, its wooden sides pitted and warped from the salt and snowy winters. Thickets and wildflowers creeped up the side. The roof sagged and was covered with dead leaves and twigs.

A terrifying pile of firewood lay halfway to the doorknob.

His shoulders sagged. He'd be in high school by the time he finished clearing out the mess. He tossed aside logs and timber to reach the door hinged on a warped doorframe, its rusted padlock open.

The chill and memories stopped Fred cold. He took a deep breath and looked back toward the house. No one followed him. He knew it. But remembering that afternoon in fourth grade when Luke and those other jerks shoved him inside and locked the door with the padlock caused his heart to race. He hadn't seen them follow him around the house or heard them sneak up to the shed until the door slammed and he was plunged into the darkness of the windowless space.

Gathering his courage, Fred snatched the padlock, stuck it in his pocket, and shouldered through the door. Hinges creaked. He sucked in another deep breath, but choked and coughed.

The morning sun knifed through the motes of dust swirling through the air. The inside looked worse than the outside, but he tried to stay positive. Cindy was arriving at noon—maybe sooner if the snotface went home early. And he didn't want her to witness him being a chicken, still afraid of the stupid shed. But he didn't want to need saving again either.

Fred had yelled himself hoarse that October afternoon, shivering from the cold. Granddad was working and Aunt Faye had kept her apothecary shop open until 8 o'clock because of an unusually large order that morning. By the time Cindy came home from dance class, night had fallen, and Fred sat curled in the dark shed crying like a baby. But now he was a middle-schooler, in the sixth grade. He glanced over his shoulder to make sure no one had followed him.

Another step.

His foot tangled in old, twined Christmas tree netting that was balled up next to the doorway. He shook himself free. Overhead, trapped fly corpses and curled-up wasps were suspended from cobwebs that crisscrossed the door frame. The sunshine penetrated the darkness only three feet into the old lean-to structure. He clicked on his flashlight.

Wood planks groaned and gave beneath his feet. Spiderwebs cocooned the old gun rack near the door. Dust sat so heavy on the plywood shelves it was impossible to see inside the line of Mason jars. He flashed the beam over the rickety wooden workbench and across scattered mouse droppings on the floor. In the right corner stood two tall shaggy shadows. Fred jumped, took two steps back and dropped the flashlight. He scrambled after it, both desperate to see the creature hovering in the corner and terrified to look.

Breathing hard, he fumbled with the light and flashed it across the shed. Two Ghillie suits hung from the ceiling on old meat hooks. Strips of burlap and twine made to look like leaves and twigs camouflaged hunters in the woods. In the dark, at first glance, they looked like monsters. He let out a relieved breath and laughed at himself for being scared. Then he coughed on the dust and musty earth again.

Hours later, Fred stood at the entrance, sweeping the dirt into a deadly cloud of mold and rodent droppings. But according to Granddad, he'd worked only twenty minutes.

"Better get a move on," Granddad said. "This shed isn't going to clean itself. I'm heading to my office."

"Still no sign of Luke? I'll come with you. Help with the—"

"No, but I'll be back 'round lunch for your aunt's chicken salad and to check on your progress. And you had better be here."

"Yes, sir." Fred glanced toward the house, mourning his freedom.

He worked for a long time after Granddad's cruiser pulled out of sight. When Aunt Faye announced that she was heading to the market, Fred declared it break time. He had to think. To figure out what happened. How could he find Luke, clear his name, and get Granddad to take the evidence seriously? Intending to return before Cindy showed, he abandoned the job and headed to the one place he could clear his mind.

From atop the raised structure, Fred stared at the familiar blue and gold circles. Wind was stronger than he would've liked, pushing the leaves in the trees to the left, and stirring the smell of grass and pine needles. He lifted his bow, nocked the arrow, and slowly let out his breath. Homing in on the black center, he smiled. That was where his shot would land.

Tension pressed against his fingers as he drew back the bowstring, one hand brushing below his chin. Ignoring the breeze that tossed a curl across his eyes, he drew in a deep breath, held it for a moment, and then exhaled and released the arrow.

A drawn-out *hiss* whizzed through the air, and then the solid *chunk* of the arrow hitting the bullseye.

Six Summit Archery Range was closer to the house, but it wasn't more than paper targets in a field. He preferred the 3-D ranges, even if they were two miles into the woods. The exact place he was not supposed to be. Wooded structures provided realism. Although he wasn't a hunter like Granddad, he imagined himself competing in archery like his dad. That was something his granddad was proud of—before his father went off trying to be smarter than everyone. Granddad valued woodsman qualities and skills. Practical, he called them.

Fred descended the rickety elevated platform and stomped down the path to the number two station. Next to tinkering with his inventions and computer, archery practice made him feel better. At least he could test his upgraded launcher with no one bothering him. But Granddad's words echoed in his mind. "Not evidence. Bigfoot nonsense. Not an investigator." He thought his granddad would be proud of his efforts to collect evidence. He always said he wanted solid proof, but he didn't.

Many attempts at a modified crossbow had left Fred low on bolts and put a massive drain on his invention budget. That's why he created the boomerang arrow launcher, but that hadn't gone so well either. He fished around in his knapsack and pulled out the repeat-bow. It was his own creation. The bow strapped to his forearm. A small lever across the palm triggered the firing mechanism.

Fred clenched his fist to reload the bolt. A mounted clip housed two dozen miniature bolts above the groove. It deposited one after he fired each shot. If he ran out of ammo, he simply had to lock in another cartridge.

He fired.

*Whoosh, whoosh, whoosh,* followed by multiple *chunks* as the arrows hit the target in rapid succession.

"Wow. What did that target ever do to you?"

Fred jumped at the sudden voice, spun around, and tried not to smile. But he couldn't help it. The last time Cindy was on the range with him was months ago.

"Don't sneak up on me like that!"

"I wasn't exactly sneaking, Freddie," Cindy said, crossing her arms over her stomach. "Did you show your granddad the evidence? My mom says they still haven't found Luke."

Fred snapped another cartridge into place, turned to the target, and emptied the clip. The rapid *chunks* didn't have their usual calming effect.

"That good, huh?" Cindy lifted his bow, rested it against her face, and nocked an arrow.

"I don't know why I bothered," he said. "Granddad doesn't believe me. He's not going to help. All it did was get me grounded."

Cindy's eyebrow raised, or at least that is what Fred thought she tried to do. Instead, one eye was open all wide, the other scrunched, and her lip made this funny squiggle. "Grounded?"

"Yeah."

Cindy's arrow flew true and struck the bullseye. She used to shoot with Fred all the time before she moved to Main Street. "Nice shot," Fred said.

She smiled and lay the bow against the tree. "So, you showed him the pictures and the fur and the jacket piece?"

Fred nodded. "He said it wasn't evidence, and the fur is fake. And said the lab would confirm it. And he told me to stay away from his crime scene. And he asked why Luke and I were fighting."

"Crime scene? So, he thinks someone—are you really a suspect?"

"Could be."

"Well, then there's no question. We need to figure out what happened to Luke."

"So, you're going to help me?"

"Of course I'm going to help you, dummy."

Fred bounced on his toes. "We could search the woods if we knew where to look. I asked Granddad where they saw Bigfoot all those years ago, but he wouldn't answer. He says Bigfoot doesn't exist. But it does. And it got Luke. I know it."

Cindy squatted on the ground. "There might be someone else who knows where to look."

Fred shook his head. "Mayor Baxter won't listen either. I doubt he'll tell us anything."

"No, not Mayor Baxter. Crazy Old Bill. I bet he'll tell us." Cindy gave him a look. "Why are you smiling like a dork?"

Cindy was a genius. Why hadn't he thought of that? "Then you believe me? Bigfoot is out there."

Cindy chewed on her lower lip. "Who said I didn't believe you?"

"You did. Then you just stopped talking to me."

Fred remembered the day. Cindy loaded the last of her things into the back of her mom's ancient station wagon and got into the front seat. He rolled alongside the car and asked if later she wanted to come over and see his latest evidence. And she clearly shook her head and said, "I don't believe you." Then she closed the window, crossed her arms, and turned to say something to her mom.

"I stopped talking to you because you're a jerk." Cindy marched through the woods with Fred trying to keep up.

"What? Wait. Why am I a jerk?"

"Move it," Cindy called. "If we hurry, we can catch a ride with my mom."

# ELEVEN

THE OLD PEOPLE'S HOME where Old Bill lived was huge. The building looked more like an English manor house than a nursing home, with massive redbrick walls, dozens of windows, and a neatly mowed lawn. Yellow, orange, and purple mums edged a wide gray cobbled path leading to an entrance with massive wooden doors. Green trees with wide patches of red leaves slumped over the roof.

Gravel crunched under the station wagon's tires as Cindy's mother pulled into a parking spot and turned off the engine. "You are sure your father will pick you up? Cause I can't leave work to drive the two of you back to town once my shift starts."

"Positive, Mom," Cindy said. "He'll meet us in an hour."

Fred hoped an hour would be enough time. Cindy told her mom they needed to interview an older member of the community to research town history. It was mostly true, except for the school project part. Cindy always said when you lie, you must stick to mostly true so it's easier to remember what you said.

They followed Cindy's mom through the mahogany doors of the old people's home. She wore navy blue scrubs with pale pink hearts and white sneakers that squeaked across the floor. Her hair was the same straw-colored blonde Cindy's was, but pin-straight and pulled back in a slick ponytail that swished back and forth.

A woman in a security uniform sat reading a magazine at a large, old-fashioned wood desk. "Morning, Ms. Thompson," she said, even though the time was just past twelve and technically afternoon. Cindy's mom had kept her married name after the divorce. When Fred asked her about it once, she had told him keeping her married name was easier than changing back to Tracy Troy on her ID and nurse's license.

"Cindy and her friend are here to visit—"

"Interview Crazy Old Bill," Fred said. "For our investigation into the kidnapping of Luke Meriwether by Big—"

Cindy elbowed him in the ribs.

"Ow."

The security lady nodded toward a clipboard on the desk. "Have them sign in."

Cindy's mom scowled.

Fred reached for a pen, but Cindy snatched it, glaring at him. She printed both of their names on the form, and in the "purpose for visit" box she wrote *school project*. He pressed his lips together. He had forgotten to lie.

Stale air and a strong smell of vinegar filled the maze of off-white hallways. Fred looked through the windows on the doors as they passed. In one room, an old woman in a bathrobe giggled at something on the television while her visitor stared out the window.

A wild-haired man popped out of the next room. Fred jumped. "My daughter is here. My daughter is here!"

Cindy's mom stepped between them and the old man. "Mr. Johnson, back in your room."

The man retreated like an automated Halloween decoration that popped out to give you a scare and sprang back to place.

At the end of the corridor, they came to a stop. Cindy's mom knocked on the door twice and opened it without waiting for a reply. "Here you are," she said, lowering her voice. "Don't be too disappointed if Mr. Baxter doesn't tell you much." She glanced at the clock on the wall. "I need to get to my station. Sara will come check on you."

Sara used to babysit Fred when he was in the second grade. She worked at Baxter's Tree Farm and as a cashier while going to the community college for aiding nurses. She always worked two jobs, three if you include watching him and Cindy wade in the lake on Saturdays. Then Fred got too big for babysitters, and the tree farm laid off most their workers. When Fred asked why, Granddad had said, "No one cuts fresh trees like they used to. All worried over the forest."

Old Bill's small room was the same not-quite-white color as the hallway. An empty hospital bed loomed in the center with a wooden headboard and a mess of sheets in the middle.

Beneath an open window sat a pale blue recliner with duct tape holding the seams together. And in it, wrapped in a plaid robe and matching slippers, sat the oldest man Fred had ever seen.

His head was bald with a few stringy long hairs white as snow. His skin, pale, near translucent. The metal stand beside his chair held a clear liquid with two long tubes that connected to the IV in his arm. He looked at them with bright blue, alert eyes.

"Let me shut the window, Mr. Baxter," a voice said from the doorway. "You're going to get sick." Sara moved past the bed and reached for the pane, dark hair swishing across her back.

"No!" Old Bill barked, and she stopped mid-reach. "I want air."

"Have it your way," she said, smiling at Fred and Cindy. "These nice children are here to see you. They're from the middle school."

Old Bill nodded. "I know you. You're Georgie's son. Joe. Or Jack. Yes, yes, Jack Moody. I'd recognize a Moody anywhere."

"Do you mean John?" Fred asked.

"Yes. That's what I said, John. John Moody."

"No, I'm Fred, remember? John is my dad."

"What? John is too young to have a boy." Old Bill squinted and leaned closer. His nose scrunched and the wrinkles on his forehead overlapped.

Fred shifted his weight from foot to foot, uncomfortable being the subject of the old man's scrutiny. Then Old Bill shrugged and sat back again. "What can I do for you?"

"You remember Cindy?"

Old Bill's eyebrows raised slightly, but he said nothing. And Fred wasn't even certain the old man knew he wasn't his dad. "We've been reading the newspaper articles from the '70s and have questions."

Old Bill frowned. "Old newspapers? It's not safe for you to go prying 'round in the past."

"Maybe this wasn't such a good idea," Cindy whispered.

Fred held out a white paper bag. "We brought you a brownie from Bigfoot Beans."

"Humph." He looked at the bag as though someone covered it with ants.

Fred and Cindy exchanged glances.

"Don't take it personally," Sara said. "Mr. Baxter doesn't like to talk to anyone."

The old man narrowed his eyes. "I'm not deaf, you know. I'm sitting right here."

"We wanted to ask you a few questions," Fred said, pulling a small memo book out of his coat pocket to jot down clues. Two of the old articles slipped from between the pages and fluttered to the ground. He quickly scooped them up.

"We're writing an article for school," Cindy said. "About town history." She glanced at Sara and gave Fred a dead-eye stare like he was supposed to know what *that* meant.

Old Bill coughed to clear his throat. "I need water." He looked at Sara expectantly.

With a worried look, she nodded and turned toward the door. "I'll just be a minute."

Baxter grinned.

Fred spoke fast. "We're investigating the disappearance of..."

"A friend from school," Cindy said.

Fred would never classify Luke as a friend, but he didn't correct her. "And we have reason to believe," he said, trying again to sound professional, "that Bigfoot was involved."

Old Bill smiled at them, but it was a sad smile that didn't crinkle the skin around his eyes. He motioned toward the bed with the crumpled blankets. "Sit," he said. "Tell me what happened."

Fred filled Old Bill in on the missing hiker, the camping couple, and the circumstances of Luke's disappearance. Granddad had called him a senile old coot more than once, but the old man listened intently and seemed perfectly sane.

"Son," Old Bill said. "That was a lifetime ago. I suggest you stay out of them woods. Nothing good lurks out in those woods."

"Please, sir." Fred held out the article. "My granddad doesn't believe me and won't go out looking for the creature." He pointed to the picture. "But this is him, isn't it?"

"Oh, Georgie was there, all right. Stubborn old fool still refuses to talk about that night. How is he? Haven't seen him in ages. Same, I expect.

Pigheaded." He studied the photo and sighed. "Look at little Jimmy. He doing good?"

"I... I don't know," Fred said.

Cindy took the news clipping and tapped the second paragraph. "It says here you went back to where your brother saw the Bigfoot the next night. But it doesn't say where."

Old Bill got a strange far-away look about him like he was dreaming or watching a memory, and then turned to stare out the window. "No one believed little Jimmy. Like you, I suspect. I went to the creek to investigate what was what."

Fred put a pen to his memo book. "Can you tell us where, so we can find our... um... friend?"

Old Bill didn't turn around. "Drove out to Marsh Trail round midnight and switched off my cruiser."

"Marsh Trail? That's way out of town," Fred said.

Old Bill kept on talking as if he had said nothing. "Heard screaming. Sounded like a wild animal or one of those ladies from the horror pictures. Bushes a few feet in front of me shook like a nor'easter blown into town, but unnatural like. There was no breeze that morning."

Gooseflesh erupted on Fred's arms. "Then what happened?" He looked at Cindy, whose eyes were round like flying saucers. She was chewing on her lip again.

Old Bill spun, making them both jump. His voice got all low and weird and creepy as if he were telling stories around a campfire. And he went ghostly. No color remained in his cheeks. "I turned on my headlights, and that must've startled it because it stepped out from the bush right on the road. Eight-foot hairy creature. My life flashed before my eyes when we locked gazes. It was pure evil. I could feel its chilly soul in that hungry look."

Sara pushed through the door, a clear plastic cup with a pile of multi-colored pills in her hand. "Time for your meds," she said, handing the cup to Old Bill. She eyed him suspiciously. "What's going on in here? You scaring these kids?"

Fred and Cindy denied being afraid, talking at the same time.

"Bottoms up," Sara said, letting the pile of pills fall from her hand into Old Bill's.

"I ain't done with my story." His voice was back to normal. "If you kids remember, I had switched off my cruiser, which I recalled when the beast started toward me. In a pure moment of training, I flipped on the overhead cherries and sirens. Bigfoot stopped dead in the road and lifted its hands up over its ears. Then turned its left shoulder down like a running back would at the moment of the handoff. I knew it planned to ram my cruiser. But its pause was enough time for me to start the engine and throw it into reverse. I peeled out just as the creature was 'bout to shoulder into my hood."

Old Bill gripped an invisible steering wheel and turned it to a hard right. "I took evasive maneuvers." The pills spilled onto the floor. He ignored them. Sara scurried after the meds. "The damn thing hit the side of the cruiser instead. Banged it up good. Had to replace the door, in fact. Half expected the car to flip, but it kept going. The creature took chase. It was fast enough to stay three car lengths behind, grunting and growling the whole time. Finally broke off north when I crossed over Turtle Creek. Damn thing just stopped and screeched bloody murder."

Fred slumped. Marsh Trail around Turtle Creek was at least 10 miles out of town—maybe more. No way could he and Cindy get to the trail themselves. And she must have been thinking the same.

"Why does everyone say the sightings were near the village?" Cindy said. "That's not even up the summits."

"Real location was kept out of the papers," Old Bill said.

"And you're sure my granddad was there? And saw the Bigfoot?"

"Hundred percent. But that Pighead wouldn't admit seeing the creature unless the whole town seen it with him."

Sara retrieved the last of Old Bill's medications from beneath the bed. "Okay, that's enough. Mr. Baxter needs his rest." She shooed Fred and Cindy, straightened the sheets, and set the pillow at the top. "Enough tales for one day." She took Old Bill by the arm and helped him into bed.

He cupped his hand, and Sara poured the pills inside. Old Bill popped them into his mouth and swallowed them in one gulp, dry. He coughed and said in a scratchy voice, "Your grandfather never stood by little Jimmy. He had no choice, understand? Jimmy had to save the town."

"All right," Sara said, retrieving a fresh blanket from a narrow closet in the corner. "You two see yourselves out. He's tired."

Fred protested but Sara had turned him around and ushered him toward the hallway. Old Bill started to snore.

# TWELVE

CINDY'S DAD SMILED INTO the rearview mirror. He had the same splash of freckles across his cheeks as Cindy, big brown eyes, and dark red hair. "Haven't seen you in ages, Freddie. How ya doing?"

"Good, sir."

"Cindy's mom tells me you two were interviewing Old Bill."

"Investigating Luke's kidnapping," Fred said. "We're collecting clues and trying to figure out where Bigfoot took him."

Cindy smacked her forehead with her palm. "Freddie."

Oops. He forgot again.

"What makes you think it was Bigfoot? Let's hear what you got."

Cindy slumped forward and put her head in her hands.

Fred opened his memo book. "First, I found a Bigfoot print out at the campsite where those hikers went missing, but it was washed away with no rain. Then, I caught the creature on film, but Granddad says it's too fuzzy to make out. After Luke disappeared, I found fur and a piece of his jacket."

"Interesting. You two are like bona fide detectives."

"And giant footprints and sneaker prints cut up the ground. And drag marks."

"How does Old Bill play into your investigation?"

"According to the papers, he was the last one to see the Bigfoot in the '70s, but it didn't say where. So, we thought if he could tell us, we could check it out. Go find the place it took Luke."

Cindy groaned.

"Hmm, sounds dangerous," her dad said, but he smiled at Fred through the mirror again. "And did you get what you needed?"

Fred flopped back into the seat. "Yeah. Problem is it's out by Turtle Creek. Too far to ride our bikes." Fred sat forward. "Mr. Thompson, you think you could drive us?"

"No can do, kiddo. Shift's starting soon. Festival weekend."

Cindy's dad was a Spanish teacher in Malone, and on the weekends, he tended bar at Talley's Pub.

"You'd think they'd cancel with a kid missing," Cindy said.

Her dad laughed. "Right, and give up all the money the peepers bring? Never happen."

"I still don't get why everyone says the sightings happened in the summits," she said. "Why lie about the location?"

"I suspect you can't sell nothing out in the sticks," he said.

"My granddad won't even admit he saw anything, so the real location doesn't matter." Fred stared out the window. Besides, it was nowhere near the place he found the evidence, the campsite, or where they last saw Luke. He couldn't shake the feeling he needed Granddad's help. Needed him to take the deputies and search for the Bigfoot and the crapweasel. But if he wouldn't admit to even seeing the creature, no way he'd agree to check Turtle Creek.

They zipped down the highway in silence. The car curved around Baker's Bend, cruising by the Welcome to Six Summit Lake sign. By the time they passed everyone in the village milling around Main Street, basking in the attention of the TV crews, an idea had stepped into Fred's view, solid and sudden, like a deer in the road. And it refused to move.

An hour later, Fred and Cindy inched into the windowless, claustrophobic storage shed, two oversized duffle bags slung over their shoulders. "Watch out for the tree netting on the—" He scanned the space. "Weird. Aunt Faye must've cleaned and tossed it in the trash or something."

"Your granddad will kill you if he catches you rifling around in his stuff," Cindy said.

"He told me to clean the place." Fred pulled the two Ghillie suits off the meat hooks. "We need to make him admit seeing Bigfoot. At least your dad believes us."

Cindy winced. "Freddie, he doesn't. He was only humoring us."

"No, he said we were bona fide detectives. He believed us."

"For a *bona fide detective*, you sure do miss stuff."

Fred shoved one suit in his duffle bag and handed the other to Cindy.

"What if they don't chase us?" she said. "What if they think we're two kids dressed in Ghillie suits?"

"They'll chase us," Fred said. "People see what they want to. They came to town to spot Bigfoot. So, when we run through the woods, that's what they'll see."

On Main Street, Fred and Cindy blended into the crowd. Fried dough and popcorn made his stomach growl. But they had no time to enjoy the food or the festival. Sure, it was stupid and cheesy and annoying—like Luke—but it was *their* town's cheesy festival, and Luke was his stupid, annoying, bullying jerk-face. There were few familiar faces. Everyone he knew was out searching the summits, which could benefit them. He was banking on out-of-towners set on spying Bigfoot.

"Ready?"

Cindy nodded.

They sprinted up an alley between Town Hall and the bike shop, and were then cut off by the last person Fred wanted to deal with.

Liza blocked the path. "What are you doing with *him?*"

"Move out of the way," Fred said.

She crossed her arms. "I watched you two dumbbells running. You're up to something."

Fred pulled air through his nose, exhaled through his mouth, and tried to sound calm. "We're going to make everyone believe—"

Cindy kicked him.

"What'd you do that for?"

"We're um...hiking the summit," Cindy said.

"Yeah," Fred said, catching on. "To look for Luke."

Liza's pinched face smoothed. "I'm coming," she said.

Cindy chewed her lip. "No. I mean, you can't. You hurt your ankle last year in cheerleading, remember? We're taking Baker. It's too steep."

"You're lying. You just don't want me to go," Liza said.

Fred pushed past the snot face. "Dumbbell."

"I'm sorry," Cindy said and followed Fred into the woods. Liza didn't.

# THIRTEEN

T HEY HURRIED ALONG THE wooded trail. Fred checked behind every few feet to be certain Liza wasn't following. He stopped next to the creek where the water was just deep enough to cover him when he lay flat on his back. "This is a good spot. Let's get ready."

Cindy stepped into the jumpsuit. "It's huge. How am I supposed to run in this?" She held out her arms. Material flopped over her wrists. The legs dragged on the floor.

Fred shoved a bulk of material into his hiker. "Tuck the pants into your boots. If we keep in the trees, no one will notice." With the hood pulled around his face, Fred was confident he resembled a hair-covered Bigfoot. But they needed to stay far enough ahead so the people couldn't get a good look.

He sloshed into the water and lay back on the cold flat stones.

"What are you doing?" Cindy asked.

"We need to cover the suits in mud and leaves, or we won't fool anyone. Now come on, get it wet."

"Great." Cindy plopped in the shallow stream, splashing water over Fred's face.

"You did that on purpose." He splashed her back. For the next half an hour, they tossed mud at each other and made water angels. They rolled out of the creek across the ground, giggling. Dirt, debris, twigs, and leaves stuck to the Ghillie suits. Mud dripped from their chins. It had been a long time since he and Cindy laughed. It was just as he'd expected. Everything was back to normal.

They waited until after five to make their appearance and give everyone time to crowd the festival. A chill wind blew, knifing through the mud-soaked hunting suits. Cindy stumbled behind Fred in her makeshift Bigfoot costume. They edged the road toward a small patch of trees near the river across from the town hall, needing to move close enough to the village so everyone would hear them holler.

"It's time," Fred said.

Cindy nodded and pulled up the Ghillie suit's dirt-crusted hood before lifting each ankle to stretch out her quads. "Let's go."

They jogged through the trees, moving toward the riverbank at an easy lope until they heard the cars and the voices, saw the rides, and the television camera lights. They had planned to shout until the news people saw them, but they didn't need to even open their mouths. First, a boy screamed and pointed. Then the camera lights pegged them near the forest edges.

"There!" a man shouted.

Fred turned and pulled Cindy in the opposite direction. They ran, leading the crowd away into the forest. He couldn't see much of anything through the burlap and mud. But he heard things closing in on them from all sides, feet stomping, twigs crunching, and men's voices shouting, "In the woods," and "get them," and "find them."

Fred and Cindy kept running, bursting through the trees, hooting and hollering, and doing their best to sound like Bigfoot.

"Everyone get back," a gruff voice commanded. Fred glanced behind him.

A man nearly blending with the trees lifted a rifle. "We've already lost one boy to the Sasquatch. No more!"

More people yelled, but Fred couldn't make out the words. They splashed across the stream, water squishing inside his boots. Branches snapped behind him. With a desperate burst of speed, they sprinted over uneven ground, trying to keep ahead of the growing mob.

Cindy was breathing hard. "It's working."

"No-talking-pace. Keep moving."

Fireworks like a blockbuster exploded. Fred flinched. Not a blockbuster. Gunshots. He may have been from the Adirondack Mountains, but he hated guns and hunting season. Charging through the forest dressed as Bigfoot—Fred realized too late—was a surefire way to get buckshot in your butt.

Another crack of gunfire. Cindy cried out, arms flailing as she stumbled and landed in a nest of thorns.

Fred scrambled to the ground next to her. "Cyd!"

She shook her head and held her foot. "My ankle. I twisted it."

"Thank goodness," Fred said. "I thought you were—I shouldn't have let you do this."

"Stop right there," Cindy said. "You don't let me do anything. I do what I want, remember?" Yes, that was the girl he remembered. His best friend.

A second gunshot sounded, and they ducked.

Cindy put her arm over her head. "What are they doing? It's illegal to hunt Bigfoot!"

"Don't think they care."

From the tree line across the brook, two figures appeared. One guy wore full camo gear from head to foot. Even his hat sported twigs and leaves. The other wore a green plaid shirt, looking like a lumberjack with jeans, boots and a camouflage hat with *BF Hunter* stitched in white letters across the top.

"Did you get them?" Lumberjack said.

"Dunno," said Camo Guy, his rifle still aimed in their direction. "Saw 'em go down."

Fred gripped Cindy's shoulder. "We need to move. Can you stand?"

She tried and whimpered.

The hunters moved closer.

Fred crawled into the thick bush and cowered. Nowhere to go. Nothing between them and the rifle-wielding thugs but trees and a few hundred yards.

"Move back farther," Fred said. "Maybe they won't peg us."

The branches of the bush hooked Cindy's Ghillie. She flailed. "I'm caught."

Fred tried to free her, branches stinging and pinching his hands. "You're stuck."

"No kidding?"

"You need to slip out of that suit." He yanked the branches and the Ghillie, but the more they struggled, the more Cindy became tangled in the nettle.

"Beneath the tree." Camo Guy's voice sounded too close.

Fred's legs shivered inside the suit from the cold and the fear. He shook his head and put a finger to his lips, motioning toward the hunters on the path.

Camo Guy whistled a little song, calm and pleasant, sweet, and low.

"Stop messing around," Lumberjack said. "Those creatures are dangerous."

"I got 'em. Beasts ain't getting up again."

Footsteps approached from somewhere behind them. Fred scrambled back, pressing closer in on Cindy. There was a crack like wood breaking, and the stench of rotting wet earth mixed with rank sweat.

Cindy wrinkled her nose and whispered. "Smells like your granddad's cigars."

The hairs on the back of Fred's neck tingled. Gooseflesh broke out on his arms, and the sudden cold seeping into his bones made him shiver.

Two whoops echoed through the woods, and then a whistle. Feral and animal-like. No sound a human could make. Leaves rustled, and the ground shook. Eerie inhuman growls and screeches came from two directions at once—from behind them and in front.

Another shrill sound, almost like a woman screaming, seemed to bounce off the trunks of the trees. Fred grabbed Cindy's arm. "We need to get out of here!"

A heavy thud made him peer from beneath the bush. He craned his neck.

A few yards to his left, eight feet in the air, two red eyes peeked from behind a towering oak. They glowed for a moment and then faded into half-closed dark orbs like giant chocolate Milk Duds. The rest of its form came into focus as if materializing out of nowhere. Its huge head reached past a high bough. Shaggy red-brown curls surrounded a hairless face. Long arms with human-like hands dragged to its knees.

The creature towered over the hunters, blocking the moonlight with its massively menacing frame. Its head hid in shadows with the moon shining at its back like a halo. Muscles rippled and bunched across the broad chest and strong slouching shoulders.

Bigfoot lumbered forward with heavy footsteps that vibrated the ground. Dark lips peeled back in a snarl, revealing a frightening set of teeth. Jagged incisors and multiple rows of canines. A deep, gut-churning growl emanated from its chest. The hunters screamed.

One huge hand went in the air, curling into a fist. Then it came down like a sledgehammer. Hunters tumbled back and a shower of dirt erupted from the ground. A row of knuckles flew toward them like a freight train. The men dove to the side, narrowly avoiding the fist that slammed into a tree.

Fred's whole body shook. They needed to run, but he couldn't move.

Camo Guy aimed his rifle. Bigfoot seized it, wrenching it from the man's grip. With a quick snap, the creature reduced it to scrap metal. The useless gun clattered to the ground next to Fred's foot. The hunters fled, sounding like an army on the move as they trampled over sticks and leaped over logs.

Then Bigfoot tore the bush out of the earth, roots and all, exposing their hiding place.

They screamed.

Fred grabbed Cindy's hand, pulled her to her feet, and ran, tugging her along. Behind them came a rustling, snapping branches, wet sucking sounds.

Fred's heart beat like wild drums. He pumped his legs faster, scrambling over tree roots and rocks.

Cindy couldn't move quickly. She limped and hobbled, crying out with each step.

"Get on my back, quick!"

She did, arms wrapping around his neck. He grabbed her legs to keep her steady.

Fred sprinted down the path, side aching, but he kept moving, each breath harder with each step. He stumbled and they fell, his foot tangled in a trap of deadwood. Cindy splayed across the ground next to him.

The thump of the creature's footfalls stopped. Fred looked at the hulking giant free to pummel them. It crouched, putting its face inches from Fred's. He didn't move. He didn't even breathe. Bigfoot tilted its head and stared. Intelligence loomed behind those chocolate eyes. Then it stood, took a few steps back, and faded into the forest, vanishing like morning fog in sunshine.

Fred let out his held breath, butt planted into the ground, trying to make sense of what had happened. His research prepared him for many things. He knew the giants were out there, but nothing could have prepared him for the fact that Bigfoot had just saved their lives.

A crack of gunfire boomed in the distance, which made his body work again.

Staying in the woods was not an option. It was near full dark. They shed the Ghillie suits, abandoning them where they landed. He scooped Cindy off the ground and headed for the shortcut.

A few moments later, he burst out on the road a half block from his house, panting and blinking sweat out of his eyes.

"I can walk," Cindy said, her voice wet.

She limped up the block, right arm draped over his shoulder, and rested on the porch steps. "Did Bigfoot just stop hunters from shooting us?"

Fred nodded. "I think so."

"It didn't hurt us. Freddie, I don't think it took Luke."

He sat next to her and studied the cracks in the sidewalk. He couldn't believe what he was about to say. "Me neither. It saved our lives." He ran his hand through his wet, muddy hair. "But if Bigfoot didn't disappear Luke, then who did?"

"That's what we need to find out."

"Like a couple of bona fide detectives?"

Cindy's blonde hair was dark with wood and dirt, making her smile look like a crescent moon in the night sky. "Exactly," she said.

# FOURTEEN

A N HOUR LATER, AFTER the ice packs and bandages, the swelling in Cindy's ankle lessened. No bruising. But she still limped a little, and she was shaking a lot. They abandoned the melted packs on the kitchen table and headed out the front door and around the side of the house, so they didn't track mud over Aunt Faye's living room carpet.

Fred unlocked the door, switched on the light, caught a whiff, and cringed. When had he started caring how bad the place looked—or smelled?

Cindy lingered in the doorway.

"You...um...want to sit?" Fred moved his dirty sweat socks from his chair and tossed them on the clothes-covered floor, scattering empty water bottles and candy wrappings from his all-nighter. He shook off his hoodie, dropping it on the chair piled with books in the corner. "You don't look so good."

"I'm fine," Cindy said and shoved the side door closed so hard one of the windowpanes shattered. She didn't flinch, only stared blankly at the jagged shards clinging to the frame like a row of shark's teeth. Then she trudged past Fred and sank into the chair, putting her head on the desk.

"I'll get the broom," Fred said, eyeing Cindy. "Be right back, okay?"

She didn't answer.

Fred returned with a broom, pan, two microwave pizzas, dry T-shirts and hoodies, and an extra pair of his sweatpants.

Tears smeared dirt down Cindy's face, but she looked better. Her hair was pulled back in a messy knot-like bun on top of her head. "Let me clean the glass," she said, reaching for the broom. "And tell your granddad I'll pay for the window. It just might take like a year of allowances."

"No." Fred handed her the dry clothes. "I'll be all right. He won't be mad. That window already had a crack. Was only a matter of time before it busted. You sure you're okay? Seeing a giant up close and personal is a traumatic event. And you're shaking, you got to change out of that wet stuff."

Cindy eyed the oversized hoodie and T-shirt and sweats and frowned. "Not going to fit. The pants I mean. They'll be way too long." Her eyes watched the concrete floor. "And tight."

"What are you talking about?"

"In case you haven't noticed, Freddie, you grew about two inches upward. I grew out."

Fred didn't get it, and he imagined the look on his face told Cindy as much.

"I gained a ton of weight over the summer," Cindy said, not meeting his eyes when she spoke.

"What? No, you didn't. You look exactly the same."

"How do you not notice anything?" Cindy snatched the clothes from his hands. "Liza never lets me forget."

"Don't listen to her." Fred felt his cheeks getting hot just thinking about the snotface. And now she was making Cindy feel bad. "Why do you hang out with her? She's...she's... not nice!"

Cindy sniffed and dragged a sleeve across her face, took the dry clothes, and went into the bathroom.

Fred swept the shards into the pan. He popped the pizzas one at a time in the microwave on the top of the dorm room fridge in the corner and then pulled out two cans of cola. He set the meal on the worktable in the center of the room and flipped open his memo pad, eating slice after slice while he waited for Cindy.

When she came out of the bathroom, she flopped into the chair next to Fred and popped open a drink. Her shirt was dry, and face washed. And the sweatpants fit just fine, except for Cindy needing to cuff them a few times. But they weren't too tight at all. Liza was such a jerk.

Cindy snatched a slice of pizza from the center of the table. "Whatcha doing?"

"Reviewing the evidence," he said, chewing around a piece of pepperoni.

"The Fortress of Geekiness turned to a detective agency office. I like it."

Fred scowled intentionally, trying to pretend to be mad, but then laughed. "So, what do we know about the kidnapping?"

Cindy's phone rang and she scooped it off the desk. "Hi, Mom... I'm at Freddie's. What's wrong?"

She clenched her teeth. "No... We didn't go to the festival, not yet, but... Why?" She showed Fred the phone and tapped the speaker icon.

Ms. Thompson's voice came through the speaker loud and shrill. "You stay indoors, understand? With wild animals running around close to town, and all the crazies wielding firearms, it's not safe. People gone out their rabid minds."

"But, Mom—"

"Don't 'but Mom,' me. Stay put. I'll know if you don't."

"Hi, Mrs. Thompson," Fred said, and Cindy winced.

"'Miss,' Frederick. Where is your granddad this evening?"

"I suspect out hunting the Bigfoot with the rest of the town."

"He should be out finding Mary's son, not chasing boogeymen."

Fred had forgotten Cindy's and Luke's mothers were friends. "I'm sure he is," Fred said. "Me and Cindy are investigating too. Collecting evidence and gathering clues like bona fide detectives." Cindy kicked him in the shin under the table. "Ow, what'd you do that for?"

"You two keep your detecting indoors. I don't suppose Faye would mind if Cindy stayed there until I'm off shift?"

Fred smiled and shoved another slice of pizza in his mouth. "She won't mind." The words came out like a garbled murmur.

"What?"

"He said, 'she won't mind,' Mom. Freddie likes to talk with his mouth full. It's gross."

"All right. I have to run before Mr. Wheeler tosses his bedpan at Sara again. Third time tonight. I'll pick you up about half past midnight."

When Ms. Thompson hung up, Cindy turned on Fred. "Why do you keep telling everyone we're investigating? You trying to get us in trouble?"

"If we're professional investigators, people will take us seriously. Besides, I'm bad at lying."

"You are. But detectives need to be sneaky and blend in. That way we can hear what people don't want us to."

Fred slumped in his chair. "I'm bad at blending, too."

Cindy walked to the map wall. "Poor Bigfoot." She sniffed. "See what we did? All the hunters will be out on the trails. They could hurt him, or worse."

"I don't know. Bigfoot looked like he could take care of himself. See what he did to that rifle?"

She sniffed again and nodded.

"But the good news is we can work on our case until midnight," Fred said. "That's plenty of time to head back up the trails and look for more leads."

"Whoa. Didn't you hear my mom? Hunters, police, news, probably dogs." Cindy glanced out the broken window. "And it's pitch dark. Not safe. Not with hunters in the woods."

"We have to do something," Fred said.

"What can we do? There's only two of us," Cindy said. "And we've made everything worse."

"If we find Luke and prove Bigfoot didn't kidnap him, then those hunters and search parties will go home."

"Maybe Luke really got lost?"

Fred shook his head. "That crapweasel knows the mountains as well as we do. Can you imagine us getting lost? Right outside O'Malley's Camp?"

Cindy's face fell. "But if he's not lost, and Bigfoot didn't take him, where is he?"

"Someone else must be involved." Fred walked over to his computer. One screen displayed the green-washed images of the creature he'd filmed a few nights before. On the other were the pictures he'd snapped in the woods.

Cindy squinted at the monitor. "Is that the fur you found?" She pointed at the picture. "It's black."

"Technically, dark brown."

"That's our proof," Cindy said. "The Bigfoot that saved our lives had scraggly, auburn hair. Kind of like my dad's."

Fred shrugged. "Night-vision camera?"

"Your night goggles wouldn't change the hair texture. That swatch is straight."

"It was soft too, which was weird. Bigfoot's fur is coarse," Fred said. "We need to go back to the camp."

Cindy motioned toward the window again. "Too dark, remember?"

"We'll use my night-vision goggles. I have two sets..." That's when Fred remembered he didn't have two sets. The crapweasel had snatched one.

He tapped the keyboard, pulling up the internet browser.

"What are you doing?"

"You're brilliant," Fred said. "I'm tracking my goggles. Remember when I got detention and didn't meet you at Baker's Trailhead? Luke snatched my night-vision."

"How's tracking them going to help? They could be in his locker or shoved beneath his bed or something."

"It's a long shot," Fred said, not taking his eyes off the screen. "But he said, 'maybe I'll see Bigfoot with these when I climb the *Drop*.' But I didn't think he was stupid enough to try it."

Fred zoomed in on the small flashing dot on the map surrounded by a circle. "Gotcha!"

Cindy sank into the desk chair. Color drained from her face like someone pulled the stopper out of the bathtub. Wide eyed with scrunched-up freckles, she said, "Is that the cave...?"

The red dot held steady in the green zone.

Fred nodded. "Up at Deadman's Drop."

The entrance to the cave didn't involve climbing the *Drop*. No one *had* to climb the *Drop*. They could take the trail on the backside of the mountain. Climbing was just something people brag about wanting to try, but no one ever did on account of it being stupid. Fred underestimated the crapweasel. Luke's picture should pop up with the web results when you search the word *stupid*.

# FIFTEEN

"FREDDIE, IF LUKE WENT to the *Drop*, no one kidnapped him. We need to call your granddad. He could be hurt or freezing or something."

Fred had the same thought, but only for a minute. He shook his head as he flipped through the photos he'd taken out in the woods. None of it made much sense.

"If Luke climbed up on his own and got hurt, how do you explain these drag marks? The messed-up footprints? Something doesn't add up."

Cindy scooted closer to the screen. "Are those sneaker marks? And..." She pointed to dark specks on the ground in the photos. "What is that?"

"Cigar butts," Fred said.

"I've seen them in a few photos. And remember the smell in the woods?"

"Cigar smoke. I remember."

Cindy's eyes got all-round and flying-saucer-like again. "Your granddad smokes cigars. You don't think he is involved in any of this, do you?"

"No way! I mean...he is definitely hiding something."

"And he lied about seeing Bigfoot."

"Yeah, but he would never hurt anyone. Besides, he insisted they go out looking for Luke and not wait for the state police."

"You're right," Cindy said. "I'm sorry. That was stupid. And lots of people smoke cigars. So, you going to call him?"

Fred flinched. "Nope. I'm supposed to be grounded. And he won't listen anyway. And well, if we find Luke ourselves, he'll take us seriously—as new detectives. Plus, wouldn't you love to see the look on Luke's face when he realizes *we* saved him?"

Cindy laughed. "That would be something."

It didn't take Fred long to fashion two homemade night-vision binoculars. He cut red and blue theatrical gels and glued them to protective eyewear and packed two red LED flashlights into his book bag. His granddad kept his hunter gear—not the guns—on the porch out back. They grabbed two reflective vests. With hunters out in the woods, they needed to be extra careful.

Cindy pulled Fred's blue hoodie over her head. "I look ridiculous," she said, holding out her arms.

"No, you don't."

She sighed and put on Fred's lined army jacket, followed by the florescent orange vest that made her look a little like a traffic cone. He had no dry shoes to fit her, so she slipped back into her wet hiking boots. "We need to take Bakers," Cindy said. "It's the fastest route."

Fred's head snapped up. "Bakers is too steep. What about your ankle?"

Cindy lifted her leg and made small circles with her foot. "It feels okay. A little achy, but I'll be fine."

"We can ride our bikes to the trail. Yours is still out back." Fred opened the side door and stepped outside.

"Wait." Cindy pulled her cellphone out of the jacket pocket and set it on Fred's desk. "Better leave this here, or my mom will know we went out."

Fred and Cindy ditched their bikes in a ramble of holly bushes next to Baker's Trail. The homemade infrared headlamp was strapped to Fred's forehead, binoculars bouncing against his chest and book bag thumping against his back.

The walking path around the pond adjacent to the entrance was suspiciously quiet. It was dark, but at least a few straggling joggers and hikers usually wound around the water in the moonlight. Fred scanned the path up the mountain, his eyes following the makeshift log steps to the sign-in box. A small solar-powered light splashed a soft glow on the warning sign. "All hikers must sign in here—no exceptions." Except, they weren't supposed to be out, and he didn't intend to tell Granddad or anyone else they were heading up the summits.

"Got your flashlight?"

"Right here," Cindy said, holding it up.

"Good. We'll use them until we run into the search parties. Then we go infrared, got it?"

She nodded, but was awful quiet, even for Cindy.

They climbed through the trail, holding trees and steadying themselves with branches. Stars glimmered through the gaps in the trees, and somewhere the moon was shining. Just not there. Branches snapped behind them, making Cindy jump. She stumbled over something in the trail and swore. "My ankle is starting to hurt."

That was what Fred worried about. "We'll need to go around and over the river. The trail is flat but longer. And then, well, there's the bridge. But...we'll be okay." He tried to sound more confident than he felt. The old bridge was rickety and in bad need of being condemned and rebuilt. He didn't like crossing in the dark, but if they kept hiking Baker's Trail, Cindy would hurt her ankle for sure. They could wind up getting to the top with no way to make it back down. "The trail that circles around isn't too much farther."

Another twig snapped somewhere behind Fred. His pulse raced, and the hairs on his arms stood on end. He looked back the way they'd come, flashing his light down the rocky incline dotted with stones and boulders. Tree trunks decorated with bits of moss marred the path. Branches and shifting shadows obscured his vision, hiding whatever was out there. He tried to calm his breathing, not wanting to alarm Cindy.

Something followed them. Getting off Baker's was definitely the best plan.

Cindy clutched a tall birch, breathing hard. She didn't seem to hear the snapping. "Yeah, okay. Let's head for the bridge."

The closer Fred and Cindy got to the ancient suspension bridge, the louder the water roared and crashed on the rocks below. Fred's heart beat against his ribs. He considered suggesting they go back, that they not cross over the river, but he was convinced they were being followed. And he didn't want to know who or what was tracking them.

The bridge swayed in the wind. Its weather-beaten planks, cracked and spaced too far apart, were lashed together by rotting ropes and rusting nails. He was glad it was dark. Hopefully, Cindy didn't remember how bad the planks looked in the day.

"Maybe we should turn out the flashlights and go infrared? In case someone sees us."

Cindy stopped walking. "Are you crazy? It's dark even with the flashlights."

"We'll be able to see with the night-vision. Besides, we'll need both our hands to hold the ropes."

"Give me the cockamamie glasses," Cindy said, holding out her hand. She slipped them over her eyes, turned off the white light, and flipped on the red LED. "It's all green and eerie."

"That means they're working."

Fred pulled out his phone and checked the steady blip on the screen. His goggles had not moved. He shoved the phone in his back pocket and peered through his binoculars. He lowered the lenses and pointed across the ravine at a high cliff jutting out over the water. "I can see the *Drop* from here. When we're closer, we'll follow the base and climb the trail to the cave. That has to be where the signal is coming from. There isn't anything else out here."

"Unless Luke's hurt out on one of the trails. Or he fell or—"

"Let's not think like that," Fred said. "We'll find him."

As they approached the rope bridge, a lump formed in Fred's throat. Beneath the rickety walkway, the silver-black water bashed against hundreds of sharp rocks cutting the surface of the river. He grasped the coarse rope handrails and took a tentative step on the wobbly plank. The bridge swayed from side to side, pushed by the rushing wind.

"I don't know if this is a good idea," Cindy said, her voice shaking.

"Stay close. And don't look down."

Cindy screamed. She'd looked down.

Fred grabbed her hand so she didn't jet across and knock them both off. "Breathe. We'll go slow."

But the farther they inched across, the stronger the wind grew.

Waves crisscrossed and slapped against each other, and Fred gripped the ropes tighter. "Hold on." His legs felt weak and rubbery. His hands hurt from the death-grip he had on the jagged line, its fibers digging into his palms. Cracks were everywhere in the wood, and the green haze of his night-vision did nothing to lessen the appearance of the gaps.

Cindy's breaths came in short huffs behind him. "How much farther?"

They were about half-way across. "Not too much to go. Put one foot in front of the other. We're fine."

He took another step. His foot slipped between two boards. He fell forward and grabbed the plank in front of him, heart hammering against his ribs. The phone slipped from his back pocket, plunging downward, splashing into the water below.

"Freddie!"

One leg dangled between the rafters. One knee balanced on the decrepit timber. He took a deep breath. "I'm okay. Hold still until I get up."

Cindy lunged to help, and the bridge lurched to the right. A plank cracked, but he couldn't tell which.

"Don't move!"

Fred gazed across the span and reached for the next plank. He pulled himself up, crawling across the boards until he was flat on his belly. He didn't want to try standing, but slithering to the other side wasn't an option. He focused on Cindy, getting her across safely. He couldn't let his best friend plunge into the icy water below. He crawled to his knees, grabbed hold of the prickly ropes, and pulled himself upright.

Together, he and Cindy moved across in slow motion, inch by inch, until they stepped on solid ground. Breathing hard, they lay on their backs, faces to the sky. Fred stared at a soaring birch tree with its bark curling down its sides, trying to slow his heartbeat. "That," he said, "was such a bad idea."

# SIXTEEN

CINDY WAS STILL BREATHING hard when she sat up and punched Fred in the shoulder. "I'm not going back that way."

Fred nodded, rubbing the ache from Cindy's fist. "Agreed."

They'd take Baker's or maybe even Peak's Trail that let out by old Kinney's field and walk the five miles back. If they had to, they'd retrieve the bikes in the morning. He pushed himself off the ground. Cindy followed, dusting the dirt from her sweatpants, goggles still squarely over her eyes, hair falling in front of her face. Between his army jacket, the night-vision, and the reflective gear, she looked like Amelia Earhart on a construction crew. The only thing missing was the aviator hat.

The bridge seemed to have stopped whatever followed them. Fred didn't tell Cindy. He was getting better at keeping secrets. Only—maybe that was a secret he should have shared. But he didn't want to freak her out. Not unless he knew for sure something, or someone, stalked the woods.

Fred peered into the binoculars and studied the bridge and land on the other side. He couldn't make it out, but a dark spot—wide and tall—rested inside the trees as if hiding in plain sight. He strained his eyes, but from that distance, it could have been anything—a shadow or a tree.

He reached for his phone to check the time, forgetting it was fish food, and swore. "I lost my phone."

"What?" The alarm in Cindy's voice was clear.

"It fell into the river when I almost...you know."

For once, he was thankful Granddad insisted he wear a watch. He had said he didn't "trust those phone screen clocks. A good old-fashioned, battery-operated timepiece is what a young man needs to keep him punctual."

But a backlight would've been nice. Fred clicked on the flashlight and shined it at the ticking hands. "We better move. It's almost 10 o'clock."

"We need to get back before my mother shows up at your house, and we're not there. I'll be grounded until I'm twenty."

"When we find Luke and become heroes, she'll let you off the hook."

"Right. Great. I'm going to be grounded for two lifetimes."

Fred's calves ached. The trail leading to the base of the *Drop* was steep, although less so than Baker's.

"How's your ankle?" His breath left little puffs of hot air when he spoke, but the T-shirt beneath his hoodie was wet and stuck to his back.

Cindy's teeth chattered slightly. "It's fine. So far."

"Be careful where you step." Fred shined the light across the path ahead, and the beam caught something pale lying on the dark ground, white against the pine and leaves. A birch or stick or something.

They stepped carefully, walking around boulders and tree roots. As they got closer to the white stick,

Fred realized it wasn't a stick but a bone—sucked dry.

And others were strewn about, piled in heaps, broken and gnawed on. Fred crouched and picked one up.

"What are you doing? That's disgusting, don't touch it."

"These bones have been here a long time," he said, turning what looked like a large thighbone over in his hands. They were almost completely clean. "And look at this." Fred ran his fingers along the length of the yellowing bone. "Teeth marks."

"Freddie, put the bone down. Unless you want half-digested pizza all over your clothes."

He tossed the bone into a bush. "At least whatever chewed on it isn't out here anymore."

"Yeah, maybe. Can we go?"

Fred flashed the light to the right. "There's the path that should circle around and rise to the cave."

They took two steps in its direction.

A shuffling and the sound of feet trampling through the woods. Cracking twigs and pinecones came from ahead. Then several bouncing orbs of light. They stood still as statues. Footsteps drew closer, heavy, and slapping on the forest floor. Someone coughed. Cindy grabbed Fred's arm. He clicked the flashlight off and plunged them into absolute darkness.

"Hey!" Cindy yelled.

"Shh," he said. "Turn on your night-vision. Whoever's out there won't be able to see us, but we should spot them. Stay close."

They moved slowly through the towering trees. Cigar smoke wafted through the air, and Fred froze. So did Cindy.

"Cigars," she whispered.

Fred turned around and tugged Cindy in the opposite direction. "My granddad will kill me if he finds us."

"But what's he doing way up here?"

"Come on, Finney," a rough voice echoed off the trees.

"Bigfoot shenanigans gone too far this time, Jim."

"Mayor Baxter?" Fred fumed. Even with their stunt, the hunters, and TV crews, people still didn't believe. He peered over the rock, trying to see if his granddad was with Baxter, but he didn't have a clear line of sight.

Cindy ducked behind a large rock. "He's with my uncle. They're probably searching for Luke like everyone else. If he sees me, he'll tell my mom. And she'll kill me."

Fred forgot the Finneys were related to Cindy. It was how he knew Officer Joe so well. He was her uncle by marriage. A few summers ago, they'd spent every weekend at the lake on Joe's kayaks. His granddad liked Joe—he did outdoorsy things Granddad approved of Fred doing. Except for Joe encouraging Fred's "Bigfoot business." But that wasn't Officer Joe's voice. It was his old man, Roy, and he wasn't as friendly.

"Keep it moving," Baxter said. "Got to get to the boy before Georgie."

Mayor Baxter always tried to show up his granddad. Not this time.

Fred slid into the tree line and motioned for Cindy to follow. They backtracked, and when they came to the bone crossroads, they circled the base of the *Drop* in the opposite direction.

Cindy tugged on Fred's jacket. "Where are we going?"

"The other way."

# SEVENTEEN

T HE CLIFF GREW IMPOSSIBLY large the closer Fred and Cindy drew to it. Fred stomped through the brush, wishing he had a bushwhacker and muttering to himself. Baxter was trying to show up his granddad. Granddad continued to lie about seeing Bigfoot, and no one even believed the creature existed. He didn't know why it made him so mad, but it did.

For a few short moments, he considered going home and leaving the crapweasel to freeze on the mountain. But Fred wasn't that big of a jerk. He had to finish it.

Cindy let out a low whistle, her face tilted skyward. "Now what?"

Fred looked up. Hair lifted on his arms and tingled at the nape of his neck. His shoulders tensed. "It's not *that* high." Maybe Luke was right, and climbing the *Drop* was not the big deal everyone made it out to be. He searched the black rock for a foothold or a notch for his hand, but found only wet stones and crevices filled with slippery moss and thorny vines.

"What are you *doing*?" Cindy's voice sounded panicked, and Fred braced himself for the onslaught.

"I'm climbing up," he said.

After the gasp, Cindy crossed her arms. "Oh no, you're not. Have you lost your mind? No one can climb the *Drop*."

Pushing back against the fear creeping up on him, Fred wiped a sweaty palm on his pants and then grabbed a thick branch from the ground. He used the jagged edge of the fractured wood to scrape away bits of moss. It made just enough space for his hand. He speared the moss and stabbed at the vines. "There's no other way. We need to reach the cave. Besides, look at the bedrock. It's got natural handholds. It doesn't look so hard."

Cindy bit her lip.

"Stay here." Fred adjusted his headlamp. "I'll be right back."

"Out of the way." Cindy shoved Fred aside. "I'll go first. That way, if I fall, I'm taking you with me."

"What? No—" Fred's words stuck in his throat. His leg muscles tightened causing them to shake. He didn't want to put Cindy in danger. This was his stupid quest, and he'd convinced her to come along. If anything happened... "You can't."

"Don't tell me what I can't do." Cindy pulled herself up by one hand. Fingers on her other hand found a tiny hold. She put her boots on a slippery rock, glanced upward, and muttered under her breath. "This is an idiotic idea."

Images of Cindy falling from the cliff clouded his vision. He pushed them aside and wiped a bead of sweat from his face. The last time he'd told Cindy she couldn't do something, she dove off Spike's Rock into the freezing lake. He'd followed and nearly drowned. And the last time he'd pointed *that* out, she'd threatened to pound his ears. Underestimating Cindy was not a good idea, but still.

He glanced back up the cliff. Stars glittered through the gaps in the trees. He hadn't planned on climbing. They had no ropes or pins to secure them properly, but it was late and cold, and if they got caught up in the woods, they'd lose their chance to save Luke. And Cindy was already a few feet above his head, so he had no choice. "I'm right behind you."

"Good. You can cushion my fall."

Fred waited at the bottom, eyes glued on his best friend, pulse throbbing in his neck.

Cindy scrambled up the rock like an expert climber, and he wondered when *that* had happened. She wedged her right boot into a toehold and grasped the rock face handhold with her fingertips on her right hand, climbing higher.

Lightning cracked the sky overhead. Cindy's foot slipped and Fred's heart leaped into his throat. He tried to call out, but his voice didn't work. It was as if everything froze, his words, his breath, and his legs—even time. Eyes fixed, he didn't even blink.

Cindy clung to the mountain wall, her right foot scrambling to find purchase. She kicked at the stones. Her boot slipped again, sending rocks falling around Fred's feet.

"Cindy!" The word finally escaped. His throat was raw from the thin air, and his voice sounded like a choking frog.

She didn't answer. Didn't look down. Her hiking boot found a crevice and she crept higher.

Fred's heart hammered against his ribs. Wind whistled along the slopes, rustling the trees. A coyote howled in the distance. Blood rushed in his ears., but he kept his eyes fixed on Cindy, nearing the top.

She clung to the rock wall a bit too long, and Fred couldn't see what she was doing. Cindy moved suddenly, and Fred's heart felt as if it had rocketed into his throat, followed by a wave of nausea. He tried to call to her, scared she would fall, but again, no words came out. As he stood there like a big frozen useless tree, Cindy's leg swung over the outcropping.

The light on her goggles disappeared into the night. The relief did nothing to slow his breath, which came out in short bursts. He cupped his hands over his mouth, sucked in a gulp of air, and shouted. "You okay?"

A small beam of light sparkled overhead. "Fine. Now get up here."

Time moved in slow motion as Fred scaled the side of the mountain. The higher he went, the drier the rocks were, and the easier the hold. He made sure he had a firm grip in one place before moving to another, trying not to think about the distance below.

As he neared the top, a smooth flat rock hovered over him. It jutted out with no place for his hands, the final obstacle to reaching the outcropping. That's what took Cindy so long toward the end of her climb, but he didn't see how she passed the spot.

"You're almost here," Cindy's voice drifted to him. "Don't stop. Keep going."

Fred knew what he needed to do. He had no choice. He had to jump and grab the edge of the outcropping with both hands. If he missed, there were only sharp rocks below to catch him. His breathing slowed as he took in the thin mountain air. The shaking in his stomach halted. It was as if all his senses went numb at once.

Wind whipped through his hair and clothes. Cindy was right. Climbing the *Drop* was an idiotic idea. He thought about her at the top alone. If there were another way, Fred would've taken it. Or climbed back down, but he couldn't.

He gathered all his strength, crouched, and jumped. The fingers of his right hand caught the top of the rock, but the other slipped, and his shin smacked against the cliff. He scrambled and found another grip for his left hand. He clutched the summit, squeezing his eyes shut and digging his fingers in the dirt.

Cindy's hands wrapped around his wrists. She pulled.

Fred found a place for his foot and pushed himself over the top of the cliff. He crawled away from the edge and flopped on his back, breathing hard and heart pounding again.

A light blinded his eyes. Cindy stood over him. "Took you long enough."

"Where'd..." His breath was back to shallow puffs. "You learn to climb like that?"

Her eyes scrunched up, and her smile widened. "Spent the summer climbing with Uncle Joe."

Fred smiled. He liked Joe.

A bird cawed overhead. Fred scrambled to his feet, wiping dirt, and sweat from his hands on his jeans. He straightened his glasses, pushed an unruly dark curl from his eyes and looked toward the sky. Nothing. Wind blew again, and with it brought a frigid cold—much colder than on the hike up. The temperature was dropping—fast.

A dark opening into the side of the mountain loomed in front of him. He motioned toward the cave. "Let's go find the crapweasel."

# EIGHTEEN

C INDY SWIRLED A LIGHT around the cave. "Luke?" The walls of the cave were wet with slime, and the faint sound of dripping water echoed everywhere. Stalactites hung like fangs from the ceiling. Puddles gathered here and there on the rough, misshapen ground, reflecting the golden light. "He's not here."

Fred shined his own light into the corners and recesses. "Has to be."

"Maybe you got the wrong spot."

"No, the GPS said my goggles were here."

But something was wrong. As far as Fred knew, the cave should have gone clear through to the other side to join with the trail. Granddad said teenagers used to come out on the ledge and mess about. He turned in another slow circle. "There should be a pass connecting the trail cavern and the *Drop* ledge. At least...according to my granddad." Fred began to question the old man's word.

"There's nothing here. No goggles. No Luke."

Wind blew in from the East and whipped into the hollow cavern. The gust swirled and rushed and whistled through an opening in the mountain wall. A moaning sound came from across the cave. "Did you hear that?"

Cindy looked to the opening. "Probably the wind."

Fred knelt and peered inside a small tunnel-like opening he hadn't noticed before in the far-right corner. Only blackness. His flashlight beam penetrated the darkness only a few feet, but he could feel a breeze blowing. "There's airflow."

The moan came again.

"That was not the wind," Fred said. "Hello? Anyone there? Luke?"

Another moan.

Cindy crouched next to him and shouted, "Luke? Is that you?"

A grunt echoed through the tunnel, and then silence.

"If he's in there, the only entrance is on the other side. We need to go back and around—even if it gets us in trouble."

They bolted back out of the cave.

Fred stood on the ledge of Deadman's Drop. He looked over the side and saw only a dizzying plunge into darkness. The base of the ridge from where they'd climbed was tucked away beneath the outcropping. The rock formed an overhang. He remembered jumping to reach the top and shivered. No way did he want to attempt that again.

He paced back and forth and peered over the edge again, trying to find a way down.

Looking like an avenging angel with the headgear halo and the glow it splashed around her feet, Cindy stood in her own tiny spotlight. Fred wished he couldn't see the look on her face—lips smashed together, eyes wide. Her arms were across her chest in                                     an if-we-weren't-a-gazillion-feet-in-the-air-I'd-toss-you-off-this-mountain pose.

"Now I know why no one can climb the *Drop*," Fred said.

"Because you can't get back down!"

Fred sighed. "I'll call Granddad. He'll alert the rangers. They'll know what to do."

"You can't. Your phone is at the bottom of the river, doofus. And mine's at your house."

Fred kicked a rock across the ground. "Dang it!" Leaving Cindy's phone so her mom couldn't track them was not the best idea they'd ever had.

The breeze picked up again, and Fred shivered. If they didn't find a way down, not only would Luke freeze to death on the other side of the rock—if it was him moaning and not some wild beast—but Fred and Cindy would be frozen kid-cicles before morning. "Let's get out of the wind. It's warmer inside the cave."

Cindy knelt in front of the tunnel entrance inside the cavern, rubbing her hands together as if over an invisible fire. "We need to go through."

"What?" Fred shook his head so hard his headlamp shifted and dislodged his night-goggles and knocked his glasses off his face. He swore and scrambled after them. By the time he reassembled his gear, Cindy sat cross-legged, peering into the dark crawlspace.

Fred squatted next to her. "I'm not going in there."

"You were right, Freddie. There's air flowing through, which means it comes out somewhere. And if that was Luke moaning—this comes out the other side. Maybe this *is* the pass."

"Or was," Fred said. "And if that's the case, and something collapsed to make it this small..." He winced. "It's not safe. And it's dark. And tight..."

"Staying here isn't an option."

Fred glared at the opening. "I won't fit."

"If I can fit, you won't have a problem."

"Why do you keep saying that? You're not fat."

She stared into the space and removed her headgear, but didn't answer.

Fred was way bigger than Cindy. Maybe his legs were a little skinnier, but he was taller and his shoulders broader. "I'll get stuck for sure."

"Look," Cindy said, pulling the reflective vest over her head. "We can't stay here. No one knows where we are." She shrugged off Fred's army jacket. It fell to the ground.

"What are you doing?"

"Getting rid of excess layers. You should too." She put the headlamp back on and adjusted the light. Then she dropped to her hands and knees and crawled into the crevice. "There's plenty of space. Follow me."

Cindy had a point. They could fall off a cliff or freeze to death. Neither were appealing options. But... confined spaces. His hands shook. "Wait," he said, but she was already several feet into the tunnel.

"Bigfoot-butts." Fred ripped off his florescent vest, slipped out of his jacket, and tugged the oversized hoodie over his head. Then, abandoning his book bag, night-vision, and miner's hat, he sat back on his heels in the recess of the rocky chamber. It was a small opening. A black hole.

Fred's heart raced. He didn't like their chances, didn't like how small the hole looked. He glared into the space. He had no idea how long the tunnel was or what lay on the other side. But he had no choice. Fixing a small flashlight between his teeth, he dove headlong into the bedrock after Cindy.

# NINETEEN

A S SOON AS FRED scooted into the hole, it was as if the crawlspace contracted. He was immediately terrified of the way the rock pressed against him, top and bottom.

Cindy looked back over her shoulder and pushed farther into the passage. She was a good bit ahead, sliding smoothly.

Army-crawling on his elbows and belly, Fred hurried forward, trying not to think about the fear. If he kept moving and got through quickly, he'd be fine. But the tunnel narrowed and forced him on his stomach. Arms straight out, he wriggled in deeper.

The flashlight in his clenched teeth illuminated the path, but the closeness increased, making him wiggle and snake his way, inches at a time. His eyes and throat burned. Cold stone pressed against his back and chest. He couldn't take a breath. He hoped and prayed Cindy would make it out the other side, get help, and save herself. Only he knew she wouldn't leave him behind—even if she should.

Fred squeezed deeper, tighter. He rocked his shoulders forward and back, pulling one leg a few inches, then the other, the stone peeling off layers of skin on his elbow. He winced at the sudden sting.

The flashlight illuminated one small area only in front of him. Cindy nearly vanished in the darkness ahead. *Just keep going. Push forward, get through.*

With the toes of his hiking boots braced against the rock, Fred gave himself a push as he wiggled. It wedged him tighter. Wetness seeped through his shirt to his skin. The water reeked of mildew and wet earth. He tried to push again. He didn't move. *Come on!* He pushed hard. Nothing. He didn't budge. Panic filled his head. He was stuck. Rock mashed his chest and back together, and he could hardly breathe. He envisioned the rock pressing on his back, the towering mountain weighing him down. Freaking out, he wiggled and squirmed, trying to back up. He couldn't. He tried to grasp the sides with his hands to get leverage. No help. He couldn't move, couldn't get enough breath. His lungs burned for air as if he were drowning, unable to breathe, suffocating. He would die, stuck in this tunnel.

Tears filled Fred's eyes, and fear gripped his throat. His toes scraped at the rock. He didn't budge. With his arms pinned ahead of him, he tried to rock back and forth. Hopeless. Cold sweat covered his face. He gasped in panic, the flashlight clattering to the rock. The tunnel was caving in, squeezing, pressing down harder. He needed help.

"I'm through," he heard Cindy say faintly in the distance. But she couldn't help. No one could.

With a grunt, desperate, he moved ahead a few more inches. That made it worse, tighter. And dark with the flashlight wedged beneath his chest, digging in. He cried. Big, wet, sloppy tears. Gasped for air. Rock crushing him.

Fred closed his eyes. A stream of tears rained down his cheeks and puddled around his nose.

"Freddie, I found him. We found Luke!"

He opened his eyes at the sound of Cindy's voice, but the tunnel was still pitch black. He closed them again.

"Freddie!"

A light shined into the dark, causing bursts of pinks and purples behind Fred's closed lids. When he opened them, it was still too bright. It took forever for his eyes to adjust. Cindy was far away.

"What's wrong?" Her voice ping-ponged off the walls.

A faint sound of dripping water echoed everywhere.

He couldn't inhale enough air to even let out the scream building in his throat. He turned his head to the side, scraping his cheek on the rough rock. But lying on his belly with his head to the side caused knifing pain to race down his neck into his shoulder blades. He pressed his forehead to the dirt, trying to stretch the tendons.

Fred closed his eyes and pushed against the rock, inching forward. But it was no good. "I'm stuck." He tried to stifle a sob.

"I'm coming," Cindy said.

For the first time since diving into the crevice, a seed of hope sprouted within his chest. As Cindy got closer, her headlamp lit the space. Each time Fred moved, the mountain wrapped him tighter like an enormous boa constrictor. He pushed with his toes.

He still couldn't move, but at least his mind worked again.

A warm hand gripped his wrist. Cindy's hair flopped in front of her face. "Can you move?"

"No. Can't...get air."

"Then don't," Cindy said. "Push it all out. Get real small. You push, and I'll pull."

She sat back on her heels. *How was she sitting?* "This is the tightest spot, I promise. Once you're through, it's easy." She didn't wait for him to answer. "You ready?"

Fred nodded and fought back the panic. What if he couldn't get any air? There was no choice. He expelled the air from his lungs. When they emptied, and he was as small as he could make himself, Fred pushed with his toes. Cindy pulled on his arms. He wiggled his body—and moved ahead about an inch.

It was tighter yet.

"Almost there. Let's do it again," Cindy said, not letting go of his hands.

Fred could not suck in a breath.

"On the count of three. Ready? One. Two. Three." Cindy pulled.

Fred grunted and kicked and rocked back and forth until he slipped forward a few inches, and the mountain released its grip.

# TWENTY

F RED CRAWLED OUT OF the mountain tunnel soaked and stinking like old sewer water. Both arms, his chin, and chest were scraped, but mostly his ego was bruised. He lay on his back in a small pool of light from Cindy's headlamp, breathing hard, his pulse and mind racing.

"You okay?"

Fred nodded, swallowing around the lump and bile in the back of his throat.

"Hang on, I'm going back for the flashlight."

Once Cindy returned, and Fred could think again, he pulled himself to his feet and shined the light around the cave. Water cascaded down the cavern walls, leaving behind frozen trails of ice.

Cindy strode to the far corner. "He's over here."

A boy-shaped lump and a once-white leather elbow of a school jacket stuck out from beneath a makeshift bear-rug blanket. He scrambled to the floor and tore the fur back.

Beneath, Luke lay on his side, one cheek pressed against the hard ground, unmoving. His brown hair hung over his eyes, and streaks of dirt ran down his face as if etched by dried tears. His body was in a fetal position, arms close together in front of him, hands in a prayer-like grip. Legs curled up. His jacket sleeve was torn, and his jeans and sneakers were caked with mud.

Cindy reached past Fred and touched Luke's face. "He's cold as ice."

"Hey, wake up," Fred said, shaking Luke's shoulder. That's when Fred realized his hands weren't in that position or his feet together because Luke was curled up. They were tied. "Help me free him."

"He's tied up!" Cindy's voice seemed far away even though she yelled right next to Fred's ear.

Fred's fingers fumbled with the twine, trying to untie the knot. There were harsh burns on Luke's wrists from struggling to free himself. Fred worked the tight knots. His mind whirled. Cindy worked at the ties around Luke's ankles.

"Got it," she said, pulling the plastic netting and unwrapping the restraints. "Who would've done this?"

"He didn't put himself in this cave. We can officially eliminate my granddad's, the-boy-is-lost-in-the-woods, theory." Fred finished freeing Luke's hands. His chest rose and fell. "He's breathing."

Cindy shook his legs. "Luke!"

Nothing.

They rolled Luke carefully on his back. Caked blood and dirt plastered the side of Luke's face, and his hair looked matted. Fred remembered the basics of the first responder's class his granddad gave every summer. ABCs. Airway: check. Breathing: check.

Pressing two fingers to the side of Luke's carotid artery, Fred checked off the C: circulation. "He's alive."

"Why isn't he waking up?"

"He's been out here two nights. Cold and dehydrated?"

"We need to get him to a hospital," Cindy said. "Think we can carry him?"

Fred slipped an arm under Luke and tried to lift, but he was dead weight. "Dude needs to lay off the burgers. We have to go for help."

He lifted the bear rug to cover Luke, but it wasn't a bear rug. "What the heck?" He spread the material out. "This is a costume." A big, black, furry Bigfoot costume complete with head and claws, but no feet. Granddad was right about one thing: the hair he found was synthetic. A patch right on the armpiece was missing.

"It was someone dressed in a costume who did this to Luke?"

Fred plucked a hair from inside the mask and held it to the light from Cindy's headlamp.

Her eyebrows scrunched together. "A hair."

The strand was the length of Fred's pointer finger. "Light-colored hair. Blond or white."

He picked up the flashlight he had set next to Luke and shined it around the inside of the cave. In the far corner stood two oversized plaster of paris feet, their soles covered in dry mud. "Looks like we found our kidnapping Bigfoot," Fred said, pointing to the impressions next to the feet in the dirt. "That explains why one set of prints I found at the campsite was shallow and had no ridges. Someone planted them." He followed another set of footprints across the room—sneaker prints.

A photo would be helpful, but his phone was gone, and the rest of his gear stuck at the other end of the tunnel of death.

Cindy pointed to the ground where Fred's light shone. "More cigar butts, and--"

"No way." Fred's words failed. In a tangled pile lay the Christmas tree netting he'd tripped over in the shed, and his granddad's Ghillie suits. "How?"

"You don't think..."

"Granddad wouldn't be involved with anything like this," Fred said, but was unsure how much he believed it at that moment. No. No. He wouldn't. But...the cigar butts, the netting, and now the Ghillie suits. Only—his granddad didn't know they took the suits. He shook his head. Nothing was making sense.

"Then who could it be?"

"Doesn't matter. Not now," Fred said. Only it did matter, he needed to push the thoughts away just then. "We need to get Luke out of here. But with him out of it, we can't exactly carry his oversized butt down the mountain. And we can't stay here either. We'll freeze to death. We need to go for help. We'll go back to town and find my granddad. He'll come back for Luke." Fred shivered. The temperature had dropped, and his shirt was soaked to the skin. "We'll need to keep moving to stay warm."

Cindy looked back. "What about him? He'll freeze if we take too long."

Fred draped the costume back over Luke. His mind whizzed through the wilderness workshops his granddad forced him to attend: Maps and Compass Fundamentals, Wilderness First Aid, Mountain Survival Skills. He had an idea. "Help me find some rocks and twigs and wood. If we start a fire, it'll warm the cave...for a little while, at least. Should buy us the time we need."

After they had collected rocks, sticks, dry pine needles, and several pieces of dead birch branches, they assembled the campfire as best they could, making a circle with the stones. Cindy peeled back layers of the birch bark and added them to the middle. Then, using the stripped wood, built a teepee.

Fred set a thin-ish branch upright with the tip digging into the top of the log. He rubbed it between his hands like a spindle as fast as he could. Using friction was the most famous way to start a fire without any matches, but also the hardest.

The log began to smoke slightly. "Put more dry leaves as soon as it sparks."

Nothing happened.

He took a break, rubbing his hands on his jeans. Then shoved them in his pockets and pulled them inside out.

"What are you doing?"

Fred smiled. "Lint."

It was only a small amount. He put the lint in the groove he'd made with the stick and started spinning it again until there was the tiniest glowing ember.

Cindy added pine needles a few at a time until they had a flame to fan.

The fire took longer than Fred had anticipated. "We need to go." He glanced at his watch. Just past midnight.

# TWENTY ONE

TWENTY MINUTES LATER, FRED and Cindy moved down the slope toward Baker's Trail, just out of sight of the flickering firelight in the cave. But the burning smoke from the fire still wafted through the night air. Cindy stopped, lifted her foot, and made tiny circles.

"Does your ankle hurt?"

"A little," she said, through chattering teeth.

Fred's legs shook from the cold. He wished they had their coats, but if he hadn't abandoned...his stomach lurched thinking about being stuck in that tunnel. He'd rather freeze to death.

Branches snapped behind them and he jumped. Then voices.

"Over there!" a man's voice yelled.

Fred spun toward the shouts. Round orbs of light bopped in the distance. A search party, and they were shouting at him and Cindy.

A small group of volunteers accompanied two rangers that Fred didn't recognize. A woman in camouflage hikers and a reflective vest rushed to Cindy with a blanket in hand. Another tossed a coat over Fred.

"What are you kids doing out here?"

Fred didn't realize his teeth chattered as bad as Cindy's until he tried to speak. "Out...looking for Luke. We..." He shivered and couldn't stop shaking. "Sheriff Moody's my granddad. We found Luke."

The rangers and volunteers listened as Fred told them all that had happened. He left out the part about climbing the *Drop* and about the evidence because Cindy kicked him each time he tried to say something. She elbowed him when he mentioned Bigfoot prints, too.

When he was done, the taller ranger stood and shook his head. "You kids could've been killed." He turned to his partner. "Get the sheriff on the horn. Tell him his grandson and his friend are here in our supervision. We'll meet him at Deadman's Cave, check out the kid's story."

Fred and Cindy trudged behind the rangers—the tall one had introduced himself as Ranger Jordan—in silence. But halfway up the path they saw that the flickering light from the fire had been replaced with floodlights. Officers milled about around the cave entrance. Two dragged a stretcher toward the crevice in the mountain. One guy Fred knew well. Tim Johnson was his granddad's deputy and a paramedic at Six Summit Rescue. But something about the scene wasn't right.

"How'd they get here so fast?" Fred shot forward, his foot slipped, but he grabbed hold of a tall pine and steadied himself. There were a few town cops he recognized, but no state police, no mountain rescue, no dogs, and no Granddad. "Did you call anyone else?" Fred asked Ranger Jordan.

"Sure didn't."

Cindy shrugged the blanket off her shoulder, letting it thump to the ground and ran for the cave. Fred followed.

Officers strapped Luke's motionless body to the stretcher, securing him with the belts, and covered him with a blanket. He didn't look good. Fred couldn't tell if his chest rose and fell. Sweat on his back dried into ice droplets. Tiny hairs on his neck and arms stood on end. Cindy gasped and her hands flew to her mouth.

Fred moved in closer. "Is he...um...?"

"He's a tad hypothermic," Johnson said. "But I suspect he'll be all right once we transport him to the medical center." The deputy squatted and grabbed the stretcher with two hands by Luke's head and motioned his partner to the other side. "Grab the feet."

The two men lifted Luke and his gurney effortlessly. They shuffled out of the cavern and started down the slope. When they were out of sight, Fred turned his attention back to the cave and the officers and the rangers and the volunteers and—Mayor Baxter?

Fred strode to where the mayor stood. The guy smiled and laughed as if he was at a barbecue. Cindy moved next to Fred.

"Excuse me, Mayor," Fred said. "Where is all the evidence?"

Baxter's mustache twitched. "Evidence?"

"The costume," Fred said. "Fake Bigfoot feet, the tree net twine..."

"His granddad's Ghillie suits."

Baxter put his hand on Fred's shoulder. "Me and my search team were the first ones on scene. I assure you none of those things were inside."

"Someone did this to Luke."

"Bigfoot did this. Look at them tracks. You know of another animal can make those?" Baxter laughed, but it was fake, Fred could tell.

Fred had the sudden urge to chuck a rock at a grown-up, which would get him grounded for life. He pulled away from the mayor.

A camera flashed, and Fred noticed giant prints on the ground. "Those weren't there earlier, and they're fake. Bigfoot is much heavier. He leaves deep tracks." He knelt in front of the apparent fake impression. "These are shallow. There are no ridges or toe prints, and the balls of the foot impressions are as flat as the rest. These were made by those plaster of paris feet that are now missing."

The mayor chuckled. "Kids."

After kicking off his boot, Fred pulled the sock off his foot. He put it in the dirt and walked several feet.

Then turned to examine the print. "See," he said. "When I walk, the balls of my feet make a deeper imprint." He pointed to the Bigfoot print. "Those are flat."

"But there were no fake feet here, boy."

"Unless you took them! You took all the evidence. It is the only explanation. And, the costume, the fake feet, the netting. Bigfoot didn't tie-up Luke."

"No, he didn't because the boy was not tied."

"We freed him." Fred's pulse raced again. No one ever believed him. He kicked a rock, sending it skipping over the dirt. "And I want my granddad's Ghillie suits back."

"What are you talking about, son?" Granddad's gruff voice made Fred jump. "Why would my Ghillies be here?"

"Georgie, your grandson's been out in the cold too long, yammering on nonsensical like."

"No," Cindy said. "When we found Luke, everything Freddie said was here is true. And he was tied up. We untied him and tried...but he wouldn't wake up. That's when Fred built a fire to keep him warm, and we went for help."

"Cynthia Josephine," Officer Joe said. His hair was long and wavy, showing off its need for a haircut when he shook his head in disapproval. "What are you doing out here? Your mother is worried sick."

Cindy's mouth moved without any words. Then she said, "Oh, um, hi, Uncle Joe."

The mayor smiled, his mustache twitching on his face. "Wild imaginations."

Fred whirled to face the mayor. "What did you do with all the evidence?"

"There was nothin' here in this cave except the Meriwether boy, unconscious, and the last embers of the fire. Smart boy that Luke, starting a fire likely saved his life." Mayor nodded his head. "Very smart."

"We started the fire," Fred said. "And how'd you know where to look? The rangers only called my Granddad. Unless..." Fred didn't want to look Granddad in the eyes. "Did you call him?"

"Wasn't me. I rushed right up when I heard you and Cindy was out in the summit mid-of-the-night."

"Followed the smell of smoke," the mayor said. "Told ya, smart kid. Lucky too. That Bigfoot might've come back and had him for breakfast."

"This was not Bigfoot," Cindy said, picking the blanket from the ground and pulling it around her shoulders. "It was someone pretending to be Bigfoot."

The mayor laughed rough and hard. "Crazy imaginations this youngin' got here."

But Granddad was not smiling.

"I'm telling the truth," Fred said. "And so is Cindy. This was not Bigfoot. Bigfoot saved our lives."

Cindy gave Fred that round flying-saucer, dead-eye stare again. And this time, he got the distinct feeling she wanted him to be quiet. Only his mouth kept going even when he tried to tell it not to. "Saved Cindy and me from the hunters. They were shooting and—"

"What do you mean from the hunters, Frederick?"

*Crapbags.*

"See," Mayor Baxter said. "Kids even saw the Bigfeets. Everyone seen the Bigfeets yesterday."

"That was us!"

"Freddie!" Cindy dropped the blanket and shoved him. "Be quiet."

"You two had better start talking," Granddad said, crossing his arms over his chest in his,

I'll-pound-you-if-you-don't, stance. Even though he'd never actually pound Fred, the look on his granddad's face was enough for him to talk. And keep it up until he spilled everything.

"And," Cindy said when Fred was finished talking, and everyone else was silent. "Sir...um...your Ghillie suits were tossed in the corner of the cave. And Luke was tied with your Christmas tree net from the shed. Or...um...someone's net."

"Could've been anything," Baxter said. "It was dark. And my boys combed this place thorough. Nothing of the sort."

Cindy ignored him and kept facing Granddad. "But the suits were yours. They were still wet with all the mud and leaves Fred and I... well, you know."

"Bigfoot running around causing havoc," Baxter said. "We'll be having to do something."

"What about the campers?" Ranger Jordan adjusted his parka. "They still missing?"

"Nah," the mayor said. "They turned up, retrieved their car from the lookout road, and headed back to where they came from. Set camp somewhere remote for the night. I told those reporters that folk ain't missing just because they don't answer their cell. Called off that search this afternoon."

A weight lifted in Fred's chest. The snow globe-shaking lady and her husband were all right. But Granddad's eyebrows crept up his forehead.

The ranger tossed his hands in the air. "No one told me. We've been out here for hours. And the lone hiker?"

"Same," Mayor said. "He's back in New Hampshire with his family. Stopped on his way home to visit some gal."

"Wish someone would've told us. Got all this manpower here. Geesh."

Granddad's expression was cold and still as a rock, like one of those presidents on Mount Rushmore. He stood quiet for what felt like an hour, but was less than a minute. He took off his sheriff's hat, ran his hands through his hair, and turned to face the trail from where they climbed to the cave. "Joe," he said.

"Yeah, Sheriff?"

"Bring Frederick and Cindy back to town, will you? Getting too cold for them to be..." He spun. "Where are your coats?"

Fred winced. He'd left out the part where he and Cindy climbed the *Drop*, couldn't get down, abandoned all their stuff, and got stuck in a mountain. He opened his mouth to spill it, but Cindy grabbed his arm.

"Let's go, Freddie. My mom is worried sick, and she's already going to be mad we left our coats with those Ghillie suits earlier."

"But we used mine—"

Cindy yanked his arm, hard, pulling him toward the path. "Come on, we're going home."

Fred looked back at Granddad, who was talking animatedly to the mayor. It reminded him of their heated conversation in the fishbowl when all this mess started. Arms flailing in the air, hand skin flapping. Granddad pulled off his hat again and slapped it against his knee. He was mad for sure, and Fred would likely be grounded until he started high school.

They trailed Officer Joe down Baker's, watching out for fallen trees and covered stones in the path. Joe had a massive flood lantern that lit the trees as they went.

"There has to be a way to prove Luke was tied up and Bigfoot didn't do it," Fred said.

Cindy pointed ahead to her uncle. "Shh. We're in enough trouble."

"That you are, young lady," Joe called.

"But you believe me?" Fred said, hurrying forward to catch the officer. Joe always believed him.

"Course, Bigfoot's out here."

"But he didn't do it."

"Don't know about that," Joe said. "No proof of what you kids claimed."

"Uncle Joe, when has Freddie ever lied about finding evidence? I mean, flat out lied?"

Joe stopped walking and turned to face them. He tilted his head as if considering something and scratched his forehead. "Never."

"Exactly," Cindy said. "So, why would he be lying now?"

"But if what you say is true, who's to blame?"

"The real question is," Fred said, "how do we prove it?"

"With no evidence—"

"Wait! There were burn marks on Luke's wrists from the twine. No one could erase those and say they didn't exist. Joe, would you at least go to the medical center and check it out? Granddad is not going to let me out of the house."

"Tell you what," Joe said, flashing his light back down the path. "I'll think about it. Now, I need to take you kids home. My sister is frantic." He eyed Cindy. "And furious."

They climbed the rest of the way down Baker's Trail in silence, until Joe veered toward the outlook where people parked their cars. "Cruiser's roadside," he said.

"But our bikes are at the bottom," Cindy said.

"I'll swing around tomorrow to pick them up."

Alongside the road, just off the blacktop, sat Officer Joe's cruiser on a misshapen angle as if he'd pulled over and hopped out in a hurry. Fred and Cindy climbed into the back seat like two caught criminals. All that was missing were the cuffs. The engine roared to life before they even closed the door, and Joe turned on the brights. Fred leaned forward in the seat, pressing close to the transparent Plexiglass divider.

The headlights revealed an area of the road several feet away. Flattened grass. There was a wide opening through the trees, and just beyond, a lump of scattered branches, piled with leaves and debris. It caught Fred's attention because it was not the natural order of things. Branches would've fallen on top of the debris, not the other way around. "What's that?"

Fred jumped out of the car before Joe started to drive and stood in the road. "It looks car-shaped."

"What the jiminy..." Joe pushed the driver's door open.

Cindy climbed from the backseat, and they trailed Joe beyond the tree line.

Joe swished the beam from his flashlight to the right and the left...and across a silver bumper. Peering out from the leaves and tree branches, part of a sticker showed. Fred gasped. It read, "Bigfoot Doesn't Believe..."

*In You Either.*

Despite Fred's protests, Joe insisted on bringing him and Cindy home—Sheriff's orders. But finding the car made Joe suspicious enough of Baxter's story not to call in the discovery over the open radio.

As the patrol car turned into the driveway, Fred winced. The front door was open, and Aunt Faye stood on the threshold in a robe with her arms crossed over her chest.

"We should go talk to Luke," he said, desperately trying to delay his aunt's wrath.

"Nice try, bud," Joe said.

"But—"

"I'll talk to Luke first thing 'morrow."

Fred turned to Cindy for help, but she only smiled weakly and said, "good luck."

# TWENTY TWO

F RED SQUINTED AT THE ray of sunshine streaming through the curtains. "What time is it?"

"Nearly nine, and you've got a visitor." Aunt Faye stood in his bedroom doorway. Her eyes puffy with sleep, and according to the lecture a few hours ago—worry. Her bathrobe was pulled closed, belt cinched around her waist, feet bare. And by the way she glared at Fred, she didn't look happy. "Up. Now. That's what you get for staying out all hours of the night and worrying me to death. Up. Up. Let's go."

"What's going on?" Fred tossed the blanket off and swung his legs over the side of the bed. He rubbed his eyes. He'd stayed awake, writing out all the clues, trying to puzzle the pieces together until the sun peeked over the mountains.

"Like I said. Visitor." Then she turned and walked out. Her bedroom door slammed.

Fred flopped back on the pillow.

Faye's door creaked. "And don't you lay back down."

He bolted upright. How does she do that? Snatching his glasses off the nightstand, he placed them over his blurry eyes and trudged downstairs.

In the foyer, Joe stood, police hat in hand. Cindy smiled next to him. "Put shoes on," she said.

"What are you doing here?"

"I did some follow-up," Joe said. "Checked on Luke. He indeed has restraint marks on both wrists and ankles. The doctor said I can talk with him this morning. Thought you'd like to come along, considering he's got you to thank for being alive."

Fred rushed to the shoe stand and shoved his feet into a pair of sneakers. "So, you believe us?"

"Never said anything different," Joe said.

Cindy smiled wide, and the freckles on her cheeks scrunched up. "Uncle Joe convinced my mom he needed my help for the rest of the case. She didn't want to, but in the interest of truth and justice, she relented. Let's go ask Luke what he remembers."

An extra puffer coat hung on the hooks in the foyer. A size too small, but it would do. Fred snatched it, shoved his arms in the sleeves, and stopped. He looked toward the stairs. "Aunt Faye—"

"Already cleared it with her," Joe said. "No worries. But there's some bad news. Baxter announced he's lifting the Bigfoot hunting ban this morning. Said he can't have the creature snatching and hurting kids in his town."

"What? Bigfoot didn't...we have to do something."

"Fred," Cindy said. "There's something else. Uncle Joe believes us, only..."

Joe put his hand on Cindy's shoulder. "Problem is what you and Cindy said about the Ghillie suits and the twine. If we find them, it kind of... Points to Sheriff Moody, doesn't it?"

"My Granddad wouldn't kidnap anyone."

"The cigars and lying about seeing Bigfoot..." Cindy said.

"I don't believe it," Joe said. "We need to find that evidence, but I wanted you to understand how it looks if we do."

He'd incriminated his own granddad. Fred's chest sank. He felt as if he'd been shot with an arrow. "Cindy, he wouldn't..."

"That's why we need to figure out who did," she said.

"Wait," Fred said. "Let me grab my notes." He ran up the stairs, banged through his bedroom door, snatched the book from his nightstand, and was downstairs and outside in less than 60 seconds.

Joe was in such a rush to talk to Luke before anyone else arrived that morning, he zipped through town with lights and sirens blaring, which caught everyone's attention. When they slowed to a crawl at the light in front of Bigfoot Beans, two kids from their class, Austin and Parker, spotted them and pointed. Fred was sure by the time they'd arrive at their destination, the whole town would think he and Cindy were going to prison.

They stepped out of the police cruiser in front of the Six Summit Lake Medical Center. Crisp air smelled of firewood and autumn. Sun beamed off the shimmering water of the lake across the road.

They rushed up the sidewalk, and as the automatic doors opened, a waft of cigar smoke pushed into the lobby behind them. "Frederick."

Granddad stood imposing and tall with his sheriff's hat tucked beneath his arm. Flight jacket with embroidered badge on the front was zipped to his neck, and his tactical pants tucked into high boots. His lips pressed into a tight line, but his eyes were soft, and forehead not as wrinkled as the night before. But the gray streaks at his temples seemed more pronounced. "What are you doing here?"

Before Fred answered, Officer Joe said, "They're with me, sir. I cleared the trip with Ms. Faye. I hope that's all right. We wanted to talk to Meriwether."

"Already spoke to the boy," Granddad said, his voice tighter than Fred's undersized puffer coat. "Bunch of his friends are in there now."

Joe swore.

Granddad sighed. "You run down that hiker from New Hampshire?"

"Talked to him this morning," Joe said, pulling a small memo book out of his back pants pocket. He glanced at his notes and chuckled. "Poor guy didn't even know he was missing. Let's see here. He said he didn't sign out when he left the trail due to being turned around and coming out a different way than where he went in. And he had his gear. So, when he hiked back to his car, he didn't bother going back to the hotel to check out either. Said stopping at the front desk isn't required."

"How 'bout that couple?"

Officer Joe shook his head. Granddad chewed on the corner of his lip. Fred wondered what they weren't saying.

"Something doesn't add up, that's for certain," Granddad said. "You kids had breakfast yet?"

"No, but we wanted to talk to Luke first," Fred said. "If...I mean...if that's okay?"

Granddad nodded. "Meet me in the cafeteria when you're done."

Fred, Cindy, and Joe took the elevator to the second floor.

Outside Luke's room, his loser friends horsed around, putting each other in headlocks and giving noogies. *Great.*

Liza sat in a chair in the waiting area with her knees pulled to her chest, looking miserable. But she flashed a lopsided smile when she saw him and Cindy. "What are you doing with that dweeb?"

"Shut up, Liza," Fred said.

"Einstein, this is all your fault. You and your stupid Bigfoot. That thing could have killed Luke. Did you see him? He looks awful."

"I saw him," Fred said. "We saved his life."

Liza rolled her eyes. "I heard the crazy story you made up."

"He didn't make anything up," Cindy said, putting her hands on her hips. "We found Luke. And if it wasn't for Freddie, Luke might've frozen to death."

Liza untucked her legs and sprang off the chair. "So now you're all buddies again? What about what a jerk he is?" She jutted her chin in Fred's direction.

"She's seen the Bigfoot," Fred said, which made Cindy cringe for reasons he couldn't figure out. "She believes me now, dummy."

"You're the dimwit." Liza scoffed. "Like she stopped talking to you because of a make-believe monster. You're so stupid."

Liza marched down the hall and pushed through the double doors, stomping her feet like a spoiled child. Fred watched her go and turned to Cindy. "What is she talking about?"

Cindy's shoulders slumped, and she flopped into the chair Liza had vacated. "Don't worry. It's nothing."

"Not if you stopped talking to me, it's not. If it wasn't because of Bigfoot, then why?"

Her eyes were big and shiny. She chewed on her lips, and red splotches appeared on her cheeks and nose. "It's just...okay. Freddie, you were so obsessed with Bigfoot you didn't notice my dad left, and we had to move out of our house. It was like you didn't even care. You were so focused on finding a giant so your dad would come home..." A tear trailed down Cindy's cheek, and she dragged her sleeve across her nose. "I wanted my dad to come home, too."

Fred's stomach tightened. "Of course, I noticed. But...I'm..." He didn't know what to say. He had been focused on finding evidence, but thought Cindy was too.

Joe put his hand on Fred's shoulder. He'd forgotten Cindy's uncle stood there. "Just say, *I'm sorry*, bud."

"I'm..." Fred couldn't breathe. "Sorry, I mean. I didn't mean to—"

Cindy wiped her eyes. "Okay, stop, doofus. You're bad at this. I forgive you."

"Cynthia," Officer Joe said. "Don't you have something to apologize for, too?"

Her eyebrows raised, and her eyes got smaller.

Joe continued. "You never told Fred why you were angry? You just stopped talking to him?"

"I..." She looked at her feet, shifting her weight from one to the other. "I guess."

"If you two are best friends, you should talk to each other. And that means telling each other when one of you hurt the other's feelings. Fred, you were unintentionally insensitive. But Cindy, you expected him to be a mind reader. And you know he's not good at that."

"True," Cindy said and laughed.

"So that means," Joe said. "You need to be more direct."

"Does it mean she needs to tell me what those dead-eye stares she gives me actually mean? Cause I've no idea."

Cindy gave him the look.

"See," Fred said. "Right there—what does that even mean?"

# TWENTY THREE

L UKE WAS NO HELP.

He still thought Fred was an idiotic nerd-brain. But at least Fred still had brainpower. Luke remembered heading toward the *Drop* because his loser friends dared him. Not too smart. He went to the woods to go pee, and the Bigfoot grabbed him. He thought the Baker cousins played a prank at first, but then the beast picked him up and made through the trees. Only thing of use Luke remembered was that "he didn't think sneakers could fit on a Bigfoot."

The next thing he remembered was waking up in the hospital.

Fred slipped into a chair opposite Granddad in the cafeteria. He glanced from his old-time newsprint and took a sip of watered-down hospital coffee out of a Styrofoam cup.

Cindy sat next to him.

Officer Joe across from her. "Talked to Tim last night. He said they were focused on getting Luke off the mountain and to the medical center. They were in the emergency room by the time they noticed the marks on his wrists and ankles. Just like Fred and Cindy said," he told Granddad. "So, me and Tim went back at the crack of dawn to take another look around."

"And?"

Fred's stomach growled, but he didn't dare leave to get breakfast from the serving line.

"Nothing."

Cindy put her head on the table. "This is hopeless."

"The answer has to be in front of us. We just don't see it yet." Fred pulled out his notebook and flipped the binding open to review what he had written before falling asleep. Puzzle pieces tried to put themselves together in his mind, but they were mismatched and slippery. He was sure the solution was there, right out of reach. "Someone put fake prints in the woods, making it look like the Bigfoot was up to no good."

Granddad winced, and Fred looked from his notes for a second before his eyes glued back to the page. "There were cigar butts at all the crime scenes. And Cindy and I found Granddad's Christmas tree netting and Ghillie suits in the cave."

"My netting?"

"The netting I got my foot tangled in when I tried to clean out the shed."

The sheriff frowned. "That netting is in the trash. Your aunt went looking for you and nearly broke her neck tripping over it. She dragged it to the can and gave me an hour-long lecture."

"So, it could be anyone's netting," Cindy said. "The whole town buys their trees at the farm."

While they talked, Officer Joe went to the serving line and piled three breakfast platters on a tray. He set them on the table and passed out plates of eggs, bacon, sausage, and over-cooked pancakes. Fred stabbed a link with his fork and shoved it in his mouth whole. His granddad was being awfully quiet.

"What I don't get," Fred said, chewing around the meat. He watched his granddad closely. "Why'd you lie about seeing Bigfoot?"

Granddad didn't blink. "Why would I?" he asked.

Cindy jumped in before he replied. "So no one would think you were crazy."

"Crazy is relative in Six Summit Lake," Officer Joe said. He filled his fork with scrambled eggs.

Granddad sipped his coffee and fixed his eyes on Fred. "I'm sorry, son. You're right. I did see the creature when I was a teen. But not since, and that's the truth."

"Why'd you lie?"

"Sometimes, son, lying is easier than admitting there are things in the world you can't explain."

"Well, Luke's kidnapping is not one of them," Fred told him. "There's an explanation. We just need to find that evidence and prove it."

Granddad glared at him. "Prove what?"

"A flesh-and-blood man disappeared Luke, not Bigfoot," Fred said, anger twisting his voice. "But what I can't figure out is how you and those deputies got up the mountain so fast."

"Fast? It took me more than an hour to hike to the summit. I must be getting old, and the cold slowed me way down."

"You are getting old," Fred said. "It took Cindy and me that much time to go the long way. And the ranger didn't call you until after we started the fire."

"I was almost to the summit time I got the call—way past midnight. I remember cause Tracy called me not ten minutes before saying she was at the house, and you and Cindy were nowhere in sight. Spittin' fire too."

Joe had said little, too busy stuffing his face full of food and washing it down with two containers of orange juice. He set the drained cardboard carton on the tray and tilted his head. He had the same look on his face Aunt Faye got when she was trying to figure out a crossword puzzle. "Tim said the same thing. Took him over an hour to climb to Deadman's Cave. It's why he rushed off the scene."

"I checked my watch when we found Luke. Had no phone. It fell in the river."

"What?" Granddad sat straight. "You lost another one?"

"I, um...yeah. But I wore the watch you gave me." He pulled up his sleeve, showing Granddad his wrist. "That's how I know the time was after midnight."

"It's true," Cindy said. "Because I knew my mother was going to kill me."

Granddad pushed his tray aside. "What time did you say Tim got that call, Joe?"

"Quarter past eleven."

"You sure?"

"Positive. Tim called Mary and told her to meet him here. She waited two hours nervous and nail biting until they showed."

Granddad pushed his chair out, stood, and snatched the flight jacket from its back. Something dark flashed in his eyes. "Go home. Now, Frederick."

"Where are you going? Baxter did this, didn't he?"

The lack of response told Fred all he needed to know. His granddad banged through the glass cafeteria doors leading to the parking lot. Fred, Cindy, and Joe followed right on his heels.

"Wait," Fred said, stomping through the wet grass and across the parking lot. "I'm coming with you."

Granddad whirled. "Oh no you are not." He hopped in the Sheriff's Department SUV without another word and sped down the road.

Joe raced to his cruiser. Fred followed. He flung open the passenger's side door, and Cindy dove inside.

"What are you two doing?" Joe said, pulling the seat belt across his chest.

"Coming with you," Cindy said.

Fred thought Joe would argue, but instead his favorite officer of the law sighed. "Buckle-up, you two."

# TWENTY FOUR

G RANDDAD STORMED INTO THE fishbowl, the door swinging so hard it shook the glass dangerously. He pinned Mayor Baxter against the wall of his office. His teeth pulled back in a sneer. "What did you do?"

"George, what's wrong with you?"

"I'm 'bout to tear you limb from limb, James, that's what's wrong. Now, tell me what you did to the Meriwether boy."

"George, you lost your mind."

Granddad put his arm across Baxter's jugular. "That boy could've frozen to death."

Fred rushed into the room. "Granddad, stop. We know what happened and have proof. Mr. Baxter kidnapped Luke and tried to blame it on Bigfoot. And we have his accomplice in custody so it's only a matter of time before he rolls over to save his own sorry butt from a long time in the slammer."

Granddad's eyes bore into him, and Fred hoped he'd play along. It was a technique he'd learned from television shows when the cops pretend the guy's partner confessed and told them everything. Neither Granddad nor Mayor Baxter knew what he was about to say.

His granddad pulled in an exaggerated breath, blew it out, and then released his grip on the mayor.

"I suppose whoever confesses first will get a better deal," Fred said. "Only a matter of time. You ready to tell your side of the story, Mr. Mayor?"

Granddad turned on Baxter swiftly, and Fred thought he'd pummel the guy. He was seeing a whole new side of the old man. "You ready to talk?"

"You're all bananas. Joe, take this crazy old coot out of here. Georgie, your days as sheriff 'round here is through."

"No sense in lying about it," Fred said. "You dressed as Bigfoot and made those fake footprints in the woods. You kid snatched Luke and dumped the costume. That's why you weren't wearing it at the opening night of the festival. I found a patch of the torn costume, and I bet it will match the one I found in the cave."

The mayor's mustache quivered. "You ain't got no proof of anything."

"We have it all," Cindy said.

The sides of granddad's lip curled upward, but only for a moment. And when the mayor turned back to face Fred, Cindy shrugged and then smiled. She gave him a thumbs-up. He continued.

"I bet when the lab processes the costume, they'll match the gray hair I found inside to you." He thought about the crime scene investigation shows. "And the saliva from the cigar butts, too."

"I ain't saying nothing," Baxter said, sitting in the office chair behind his glass-top desk.

"Won't matter," Fred said.

Officer Joe moved in front of the door and crossed his arms, blocking the mayor's only escape route. Not that Fred thought he'd make a run for it, but still, Joe's barrel chest blocking the exit was comforting.

Fred turned to his granddad. "The mayor was out in the woods planting footprints to cause Bigfoot hysteria. Old Bill told us he had to save the town. And Baxter himself extended the festival so more peepers would come and spend money. No Bigfoot. No Peepers."

"But why kidnap a kid?" Officer Joe demanded.

"Because Luke saw him doing it," Fred said, enjoying the shock on granddad's face. "Luke remembered Bigfoot wearing sneakers, and the costume we found had no feet. So, the Mayor's sneakers would've been showing. I bet the soil match will check out too if we confiscate the sneakers he's wearing. Only Mayor Baxter didn't realize the crapweasel swiped my night-vision goggles in school, and I had a tracker device attached to them."

Granddad frowned. "You didn't mention that."

"Sorry," Fred said. "I forgot until me and Cindy needed them to go looking for Luke."

Baxter jolted out of his seat. "I'm not listening to any more of this nonsense."

Granddad blocked his path.

"Out of my way, Georgie."

"Sit, or I'll make you sit."

"Come on, Baxter," Fred said. "You might as well tell us what happened before your buddy does."

Baxter glared at him, his pale face blank. "What buddy?"

"You knew Luke was in the cave, and it was getting freezing up on the mountain, so you had to orchestrate his rescue just right. Temperature dropped too fast, so you called for the med crew and deputies before you got to the summit. Those calls went out little after eleven, but we found Luke after midnight, and you weren't there yet."

"Only someone who knew where the boy was could do that," Granddad said. He glanced at Fred. "I'm sorry I didn't believe you."

"And for sure, he couldn't do all this alone," Joe said.

"If you knew what you was talking about, Officer Doodleshnitzer," the mayor said, a smirk on his face. "You'd not be smiling."

That's when Fred was certain he was right. He sighed. On some level, he hoped for Joe and Cindy's sake he wasn't.

"How'd you remove the evidence so fast? All the deputies on the scene swore nothing was there when they arrived. They got the call to come up, but none of them were first on scene. Baxter, you were."

Fred didn't want to smile, so he did his best to keep a stone face. "Because Baxter's accomplice wasn't on the scene, he already left with the evidence. Isn't that right? Me and Cindy heard them talking."

Cindy gasped.

Joe scratched his head. "What's he talking about?"

"When Fred and I hiked up, we planned to take the path to the cave, but we heard Baxter out there looking for Luke and ducked into the bushes. That's why Fred and I went the other way and climbed the stupid *Drop*. Didn't want Uncle Roy to see me and tell mom we were out there."

"You what?" Joe said, his arms flying in the air.

Fred laughed. "You told me not to say anything, and you spilled the beans this time."

"Not funny." Cindy did the dead-eye again. She blew out a breath and looked at her uncle. "He was there. So, when Mayor Baxter said he found Luke because of seeing the smoke from the campfire, we didn't think much of it."

"Until all the evidence went missing," Fred said. "And the deputies got there so quick."

"With all the commotion, I didn't realize Uncle Roy wasn't with the rescue crew."

Officer Joe looked as if he'd be sick. "He might've got away with it, too. Had he not called the cavalry in advance."

"This is all your fault, Georgie," Baxter said. "If you waited for the state police, I could've fetched the boy. But you brought everyone in, and I had to wait all this time. If the boy is hurt, it's your doing."

Granddad looked at Joe apologetically. "You know what I need to do, son, right?"

Joe nodded. "Yes, sir. I'll come with."

"No, I've got this. I'll bring the kids home first. Put Baxter in lock-up until the state can pick him up."

Granddad cuffed Mayor Baxter's hands behind his back. "One more thing. What'd you do with that couple who came to hike and camp peacefully?"

"I done nothing with those folks." A clench of granddad's hand on the cuffs caused the mayor to wince. "I had to get the Staties out the summits to get to the Meriwether boy. All I done was hide the car and call off the search. Temporarily, of course. Just til the boy was safe, you understand."

Fred shifted his weight and bounced on his toes, both from being nervous about what might've happened to them and eager to help. "So, they're still missing?"

"Gone without a trace," Baxter said, turning to Granddad. "You know that happens here, Georgie."

Officer Joe took hold of the mayor by his elbow, guiding him toward the glass door of the fishbowl office.

Tears slid down Cindy's cheeks. "I'm sorry, Uncle Joe."

"You've got nothing to be sorry about. You and Freddie both did good."

Granddad put a hand on each of Fred's shoulders and looked him in the eyes, which was totally uncomfortable. But Fred tried not to look away.

"I'm proud of you, son. What you did was very brave," Granddad said. "Dangerous. But brave."

# TWENTY FIVE

THE MISSING EVIDENCE TURNED up in Sergeant Finney's garage. Newspaper people came from as far as Washington D.C. to cover the Bigfoot scandal, plastering Baxter's and Finney's arrests all over the front pages. But the good news was the creature was in the clear. Everyone went back to not really believing Bigfoot roamed the summits.

Cindy set the cauldron filled with candy on the porch steps and sighed. "You solved a kidnapping. I can't believe you got grounded."

Fred had spent the whole month working on his latest invention—an automated Halloween candy dispenser—and researching exactly how many people went missing in the summits. Since the first Bigfoot sighting involving his granddad, there had been sixty-eight, nearly two per year. Much of the

Adirondack Mountains are protected, forever-wild, lands, making them dangerous to navigate, but still, Fred thought that was a huge number. Not all the disappearances were from the woods around the summits, or that would've drawn attention. They were spread out over the larger area—but not too large of an area.

He had hoped to find a clue as to what may have happened to the snowglobe-shaking lady and her husband. No luck.

Fred sat on the step and stared at the plastic tombstone in the front yard. Since it was the first day Fred was allowed back into society, Cindy came by at 8am. They spent the day decorating, making Fred's place its usual haunted house attraction for the little ones. Fake blood-soaked hands reached from between Aunt Faye's potted mums. Webs crisscrossed the doorframe, glow-in-dark skeletons dangled. Small speakers lining the porch railing played eerie sounds. As the sky faded to indigo, the streetlights had popped on along with the solar-powered green and purple skull heads, illuminating the path to the front door.

Fred switched on the fog machine Cindy had borrowed from the high school's theater department and smiled. He plugged his Insta-Candy-Giver-Outer into the extension cord, and it whirled to life. The idea was simple. Load candy into the funnel at the top, and when the pedal is pressed—which was halfway up the walkway connected by a thin wire—it pitched candy at the trick or treater.

"I downloaded Monster Mash music to set the mood," Cindy said, tapping the Bluetooth function on her phone. The classic Halloween song blared from the speakers. "Much better."

In typical Cindy fashion, she'd turned their creepy graveyard into something fun and upbeat. Strings of purple and white lights twinkled on the bushes, splashing light on her bright green, turquoise, pink, and purple sparkly fairy costume.

"I thought you were going to be a witch?"

"Witches. Fairies. They both have magic. And what are you supposed to be?"

He rolled his eyes. Girls. He hoisted a wooden beam, pointed at one end over his head. "Can't you tell? I'm a giant hunter."

"You can't stake a giant," Cindy said. "They're not vampires. Besides, you wouldn't hurt Bigfoot."

"No, not him. But there are others, and they're vicious." Fred pointed the tip into the lawn and pushed down. It bent as easily as a blade of grass. "It's fake anyway," he said, tossing it aside and sitting on the top step. As he plucked Charleston Chews from the candy cauldron, he heard a voice he could not mistake.

"If it isn't nerd-brain and his nerd-girl," Luke said, as his imbecile side-kick James laughed hysterically. "Hanging out with Bigfoot again? I thought I smelled something skunky."

Behind Luke, the klepto-snot face, Liza, snorted.

Fred stood and walked down the steps toward the crapweasel. "It's your BO, Luke." He flinched away when the brainless dummy tried to slap him across the top of his head before lurching forward and digging into the treats, triumphant.

"You're such a jerk," Cindy said. "And get out of the candy. That's for the little kids."

"Luke *is* one of the little kids," Fred said.

"Whatever." Luke snatched another handful of loot and walked away to harass another group of kids.

Liza shook her head at Cindy in disapproval. "You're pathetic," she said. "I can't believe you chose *him* over us, Cynthia. Honestly."

"Any day of the year, Liza." Cindy smiled almost too sweetly, which made Fred suspicious. She lifted the cauldron of candy and shook a pile into the funnel at the top of Fred's Insta-Candy-Giver-Outer.

Undeterred, Liza stalked toward Cindy and stepped on the hidden foot pedal. The machine whirled louder. Then it launched a piece of candy at Liza as Fred had designed it to. Only—it kept pitching.

"Ow! Ow," Liza said, backing away, "make it stop!"

Cindy was laughing too hard to stop the candy assault.

As Liza scurried down the street after Luke and those jerks, Fred's front door opened.

"What's going on out here?" Granddad stood like a thin birch between two oaks in the door frame. His sheriff's hat tucked beneath his arm and jacket hanging open. He glanced toward Fred's machine still chucking candy onto the front path. "Needs some adjustments, son?"

"Yes, sir."

"Better get to it."

"10-4," Fred said. "Hey, where's your cruiser?" Without the car in the drive, Fred had not realized Granddad was at home.

"Getting the brakes done."

The first wave of small ghouls and goblins ran toward the house as Officer Joe pulled to the curb. "You ready, Sheriff?"

Granddad hurried toward the car.

"Where you going?" Fred asked, following in his granddad's hurried pace.

"Got a car accident out on the eighty-six." Joe leaned toward the window and winked. "Get this...they say Bigfoot ran them off the road."

"We should come with you," Fred said, bouncing on his toes.

"No," Granddad said, firmly. "No more messing about in police business, you hear?"

"But, if it's Bigfoot—"

"Frederick." Granddad's tone turned dangerous. Fred was in grave danger of being grounded again.

"Come on, Sheriff. The crash *is* out by Turtle Creek across from Marsh Trail."

Granddad's face went ghostly.

Joe laughed. "I'm just messing with you. It's right past the Squeaky Nail on 86."

But his granddad did not look amused. "I'll be back when I'm back."

"Trick or Treat!" A little goblin looked up at Fred, who dropped a handful of candy in his bag. "Thanks!"

But Fred wasn't paying much attention.

"Oh, no," Cindy said. "I know that look."

"We need to check it out," Fred said, heading for the house.

"You just got off grounding. This is what got you in trouble to begin with."

"But I've got you to get me out again," he said, pulling at Cindy's arm. "We'll take the bikes. Joe dropped them by last week."

"This is a bad idea, Freddie." Cindy took off her fairy wings and set them on the porch.

Fred rushed up the front steps, swung open the front door, and nearly knocked over Aunt Faye. "Can you give out the candy for a bit? Me and Cindy are going to take a bike ride."

"Of course." Aunt Faye shooed Fred aside, stepping out on the porch and twirling as if walking a fashion runway. Her midnight-blue evening gown twinkled with yellow sequined stars. Her long, dark braid with silver streaks hung over her shoulder. The bright green pointy hat atop of her head did not match the rest of the outfit. Sticking out from beneath her dress were green-and-purple striped tights with bath slippers. "What do you think?"

"Um..." Fred said. "Bath slippers look ridiculous with the dress."

Cindy kicked him.

"Ow. What'd you do that for?"

"It's very cool, Miss Faye," Cindy said, tilting her head toward Fred and then lifting it toward his aunt—like he was supposed to know what *that* meant.

"Thank you, Cynthia," Faye said. "Where are you running off to?"

"We need to check out the crash. It could be a giant sighting."

"Freddie!" Cindy's eyes narrowed and her brows did that weird scrunchy thing.

Aunt Faye's smile disappeared. "Frederick," she said in a warning tone that made him feel like a squirming second grader. "Stay out of the woods after dark. It's not safe. Besides, killing giants requires sunshine."

"Don't worry, Aunt Faye," Fred said, smiling widely. "Bigfoot is harmless."

His aunt looked at him real serious and said, "Bigfoot is not the only thing that lives in these mountains." And before Fred could ask her what she meant, Faye whooshed past him with a bucket of Halloween candy. "Oh look, more goblins!"

Fred made for the Watchcave. "Let's get going."

"Wait." Cindy grabbed his arm. "What did Faye mean, *not the only thing that lives in these mountains?*"

"Bears, mountain lions..." Fred stopped mid-step and spun around. "Did she say *killing giants?*"

# Acknowledgments

Birthing a book is like raising a child—it takes a village. Many people helped create this book, and I am grateful to each of them.

Frederick Moody is a character that has lived in my head for a long time—go-go-gadget Fred—is what I used to call him. He was spunky and brave and brilliant and very misunderstood. He misinterpreted social cues and people in general, often to comic effect and complications in his life. I see reflections of myself and my boys in Frederick—all of whom are on the autism spectrum, and it is my greatest hope that kids that are a little bit different can see themselves and how wonderful they are reflected in Fred's stories.

So, my first thanks go to all my boys, Adam, Matthew, Thomas, and Jason, who sacrificed Mommy-time so that I could write. And to my husband, Mark, without whom none of this would be possible. Thank you for all the dishes and dinners and tackling of the kids before they busted into my office while I was working. And for reading all my awful drafts. I love you all very much.

About that village—Frederick would not have been able to come alive on the page without the MFA program at Seton Hill University, my mentors, critique partners, and dear friends. To my SHU mentors: Jason Jack Miller, thank you for believing in me when I clearly lacked confidence in myself. Will Horner, thank you for your support. I cannot tell you how thankful I am for all the work you put into Fred and Cindy, and how you cheered the project on. Thank you to the wonderful critique partners, Tacoma, Kelsie, Johnnie, Felicia, Rasheedah, and Diane, who each had a hand in making every word on these pages better than I could have done on my own.

To my dear friend, Rosanna, thank you for always being there, and for our daily talks that have often backed me away from the fireplace when I wanted to toss in all the manuscript pages and watch them burn.

To my friend, critique, and writing partner, John. You have been instrumental in holding these stories together. I appreciate all your time, editing, cover design, and support you have for my work. I could not have done it without constant support and encouragement, and your refusal to let me be lazy and leave these stories in the drawer. Thank you is not enough.

And of course, thank you to all of you for joining Fred on his wacky, giant-hunting adventure!

*Jeannie*

# ABOUT JEANNIE

Jeannie Rivera is the award-winning author of *Twirling Naked in the Streets, and No One Noticed*: *Growing Up With Undiagnosed Autism*, and *Frederick*  *Moody and the Secrets of Six Summit Lake*. She splits her time living in the Adirondack Mountains of New York and sunny Florida with her husband, their four boys, dog, and two cats.

**jeannierivera.com**
**Twitter: @AspieWriter**

# ALSO BY JEANNIE

**Amazon Kindle # 1 Best Seller in**
**Communicative Disorders**
**2013 International Reader's Favorite Silver**
**Award Winner**

Jeannie grew up with autism, but no one around her knew it. Twirling Naked in the Streets will take you on a journey into the mind of a child on the autism spectrum; a child who grows into an adolescent, an adult, and  becomes a wife, mother, student, and writer with autism.

This is a gripping memoir of a quirky, weird, but gifted child who grows up never quite finding her niche only to discover at the age of 38 that all the issues, problems, and weirdness she experienced were because she  had Asperger's Syndrome (AS), a form of high-functioning autism.

**Available in print and ebook at Amazon.com**